Sparked
The Legends of Silver Grove
Amanda Penn

This is a work of fiction. Similarities to real people, places, or events are entirely coincidental.

SPARKED

First edition. July 13, 2023.

Copyright © 2023 Amanda Penn.

ISBN: 979-8223343264

Written by Amanda Penn.

For my daughter, Izzie Penn. Thank you for supporting me and cheering me on. I love you more. (Now it's in print so I win.)

Chapter One

She sat on the top step of the porch as the chill of the concrete seeped through her clothes and into her skin, penetrating through her muddled memories. A chill slid down her spine, the coolness of the air offering some solace as she tried to understand what had happened inside the frat house.

High-pitched, hysterical voices from inside blended with the chirping of crickets, becoming a dull roar in her head. She lifted a trembling hand to brush the golden blonde hair from her sweat-drenched cheeks, then paused with her fingers spread in front of her.

Her eyes widened at the crimson stains covering the smooth skin. The metallic scent cut through the sweet aroma of honeysuckle, reminding her of what she had done. Though how she had done it remained a mystery.

"Ma'am?"

She blinked rapidly as the authoritative voice broke through the dull roar in her mind. She raised her head to find a police officer, his hand on his gun at his hip, his sharp gaze regarding her with suspicion.

He stood on the sidewalk a few feet from her, the light from the streetlamp above slicing through the night. He regarded her with the same caution someone would give a wild animal.

She stared at him, then his hand poised over his weapon. Did he think she was the danger?

"Yes?" she asked, her voice dull as she continued to regard him with shock-filled cerulean eyes.

She moved to lower her hand, but the officer stiffened, tightening his grip on the handle of his gun, the hair on her nape standing on end in warning.

"Don't move," He ordered, his stern voice causing her to pause. She nodded, swallowing, her stomach roiling as he took a wary step toward her. "What's your name?" he asked, his voice both demanding and professional.

She stared at him, perplexed, taking in his words before she realized she should answer.

"B-Brianna...Brianna Powers," she stammered as a shiver worked through her.

"Are there others inside?" he asked, his brow furrowing over his weathered features.

She straightened and glanced behind her as the door to the fraternity house swung open. Swallowing, taking in the dark shadows of the people within, she realized she never should have come. Her mother had told her not to, even when her father had encouraged her to attend. It had been too dangerous for a sixteen-year-old girl. Her mother was right.

"Yes, there are others inside," she said as a tear fell from her eye and trickled down her cheek because at least one of them was dead. She tried to push away the memory of the girl lying in the middle of the floor, pale and unmoving from her mind.

The door opened wider, illuminating the porch in the pale light from inside as a girl scrambled out, surprising the policeman when she flung herself into his arms, sobbing. He held her as she cried, her body shaking. His eyes widened in bewilderment as others filed out of the house, their faces ashen from the terror that had befallen them inside.

Brianna swallowed as her memory offered the moment the frat boys grew fangs and their formerly handsome faces stretched into something terrifying. She shook her head, banishing the memory.

"Can someone tell me what happened?" The police officer asked, his voice edged with worry. He glanced over the girl's head toward the group walking down the porch steps.

A blond guy with the build of a football player who Brianna vaguely recollected his name as being Brett answered, "T-They tried to kill us," he said, his voice cracking. "The guys who live here tried to kill us."

Brianna trembled as another memory floated to the surface of her mind unbidden. The male voice in her head, ordering her to fight, telling her exactly what to do as one of the monsters reached for her. She took a deep breath, forcing the memory away.

Am I insane? She shook her head, denying it. She tried to convince herself that the voice had come from the overwhelming fear of dying, but she knew it didn't. The voice had come from something else.

"How?" The officer gestured to another girl, who walked up to him and took the sobbing girl from his arms, then stepped closer to Brianna and the guy who had spoken.

"They're monsters," Brianna said softly, her voice monotone. She squeezed her eyes shut, realizing that it sounded crazy, but it was the truth. She witnessed their faces changing. "They tried to drain our blood...T-to drink it."

The officer unholstered his weapon, motioning everybody off the porch so he could see inside. "Are they still in there?"

He took his eyes off Brianna. Obviously, he no longer thought she was a threat.

"No," Brett answered, pointing at her with a long, thick finger as his voice trembled. "She f-fought them. They ran away."

The police officer took in Brianna's blood-stained clothes, and the crimson marks splattered on her face before noticing her slight frame. "She helped fight them?"

Brett shook his head as he glanced between Brianna and the officer, his eyes wide. "No, she fought them on her own. She saved our lives."

"How?" the officer asked, eyes narrowed.

She shook her head as she whispered, "I don't know."

She raised her hand to her head as the world around her grew dim. At that moment, she was sure her sanity was slipping because she heard another voice...a soft, feminine one whisper, "Sleep now."

Darkness clouded her vision as Brett leaned down to catch her before she could hit her head against the hard surface of the porch as the bloody night of monsters and death became too much.

She closed her eyes and gave in to the comfort of darkness where nothing could hurt her, and she didn't have to protect anyone else.

-THREE MONTHS LATER

Brianna opened her eyes, blinking away sleep as she found herself in a barren, white hallway. Clear plastic covered the doors, fluttering in the breeze, drifting in from the open windows.

Brows furrowed, she tip-toed forward on bare feet, crossing the cold marble floor and shivering as the wind penetrated her thin nightclothes, swirling the musty scent of disuse around her.

She crossed her arms over her chest, hugging her elbows as she took one hesitant step after another, trying to remember how she had come to be there.

Muted voices from one of the rooms at the end of the hallway beckoned her closer.

"We're going to get caught," a girl whispered, her voice quivering.

"No, we won't," a male responded. His voice rose louder than the girl's, as if to prove his point.

"Shhh...I don't want to get kicked out," the girl pleaded, keeping her voice low. "My parents would kill me. You didn't tell your friends you were meeting me, did you?"

"No, I didn't. They wouldn't believe me." He chuckled.

"I'm sorry. I just don't want someone telling on us. I know you think it's silly, but I don't want to get kicked out," she said, the quiver in her voice echoing down the hall.

"Even if someone found us here, I doubt they would kick you out," he laughed, as if the thought of it was ludicrous. "What are you afraid of? Me?"

"N-No," the girl stuttered as Brianna tiptoed closer. "Are you sure no one will find us?"

"I'm positive."

There was a beat of silence before the girl answered with a breath of relief. "Okay."

That one word sent a chill down Brianna's spine. It was the same feeling she had a moment before the fraternity guys had locked everyone in that room on the most terrifying night of her life and drained a girl who was a little older than herself of blood with fangs that were far from human. It was what had spurred her to fight them off... Well, that and a voice she couldn't explain.

She bolted toward the door, hoping she could prevent whatever tragedy was about to take place, but before she got half-way there, she heard the boy scream.

"What are you doing?" His voice now held terror, far from the humor he had exuded moments before. Something crackled beyond the doorway before the hall was aglow in bright orange, the acrid scent of smoke reaching her.

Brianna reached for the plastic hanging between the room and the hallway, but it melted away as flames licked the doorframe, bubbling the paint there and turning it black. Her heart raced as she became desperate *to save the two people trapped within, but then the flames faded, shrinking away from the door.*

She frowned, tilting her head as she stared at the door. She had never seen flames react the way those had.

Taking a tentative step forward, she peered inside, expecting to see the boy and the girl huddled in the corner. She gasped, placing a hand over her mouth as her stomach churned, threatening to empty its contents.

In the center of the room lay the boy, his black, charred skin melting from his body, his face frozen in a scream.

Her eyes flew open as she suppressed a scream that begged to be released. Her gaze flew around the room before she let out a shaky breath, seeing she was still in her bedroom in her mother's new house. She swiped her hand over her eyes, trying to relieve the burning of hot tears mixed with the abrasive heat left by the smoke.

"Brianna, breakfast is ready!" her mother called from the kitchen downstairs, her voice too cheerful for the dream Brianna just had.

Brianna glanced around the room that was hers on the weekends and holidays. She would spend every other day at the boarding school across town.

She rose from the bed as tears burned her eyes, trying to convince herself her nightmare was from the anxiety of starting a new school, nothing else. She glanced at the uniform hanging on the hook on the back of her door. The crest on the right breast was the likeness of Medusa's head in silver with the words, *In tenebris ego sum forti.*

"In the darkness, I am brave," she whispered, closing her eyes, hoping that the motto would give her the bravery she needed because lately, everything seemed shrouded in a thick cloud so dark she couldn't see beyond it.

BRIANNA STARED OUT the window as they passed mansions surrounded by tall palm trees. Her eyes darted from them to her mother.

She found it hard to picture her mother there amongst the richest people of California. She had always appeared happy to live in their modest, middle-class neighborhood, but that was before her parents' divorce.

Her heart should have been broken with the news that broke their family in two, but her father rarely noticed her presence unless he was trying to undermine her mother. Then, he used her and her sister, Sadie, to enact whatever revenge he felt his wife deserved. So, the only pain Brianna experienced during the divorce happened when he asked for Sadie to stay with him until she was sixteen and didn't ask the same for Brianna. It made her bitter towards him because no matter how he treated her, she always hoped he loved her. That action proved otherwise.

Until that rejection, her mother never spoke of her life before marrying her father. It wasn't until what happened at the frat party that Brianna learned anything about her mother's past and that was only because Brianna needed a fresh start away from everyone who knew what happened.

"Mom, how did you get accepted into Silver Grove?" Brianna asked, glancing at the view beyond the car.

"I guess the same way you did," she said, shrugging, capturing Brianna's attention because, for once, she seemed willing to give her information. Her blue eyes sparkled, but something in her voice made Brianna wonder if she was lying. "I got a scholarship. Only very special people get them."

"And you're special?" she asked, narrowing her eyes. It wasn't in Juliette Powers' nature to brag, but she hoped her mother would continue telling her things about her youth.

"I don't think I am," she sighed, but a small smile played across her lips. "But they did, and I was happy to be there."

"Why?" Brianna asked, wanting to dispel the worry and nervousness that had settled in the pit of her stomach. She couldn't get rid of the sense that Silver Grove Academy was the start of something she didn't comprehend.

"I never fit in," she said, her gaze narrowing on the road in front of her. "I mean... I had friends, but I always felt... different. Everyone else always enjoyed love and light, but I loved rawer, darker things. At Silver Grove Academy, I was a puzzle piece that fit."

Brianna smiled because she understood. She always found as much solace in the dark as the light.

The tension in her shoulders relaxed when the scenery began to change, large California pines dotting the road before leading into a forest thick with them. A woodsy scent surrounded her, the aroma pleasant. It was strange to go from palm trees to evergreens.

Sighing, she glanced at her mother, her brows furrowing. "Are we still in Silver Grove?"

"We are, but the school is on the outskirts of town." She smiled. "They want to remain undisturbed by neighbors, so they have a lot of land."

"Oh."

Brianna stared out the window again. The forest started to thin, ending at a gray, stone wall so tall she couldn't view anything beyond it. A man strolled along the sidewalk beside the wall. He turned toward them as they approached. He wore a business suit that hugged his athletic frame. Ebony hair was combed away from his hard face. Though he didn't seem angry, Brianna sensed the hate radiating from him.

"Mom, do you see that man?" But when she blinked, he was gone. She looked over her shoulder, her eyes moving frantically in search of him, but he was nowhere to be found.

Her mother stopped in front of a wrought-iron gate; Medusa's head etched across the front. Brianna's previous question went unheard.

She shook her head, trying to convince herself that the man she saw had been in her imagination. But instead of calming her, a tremble slid down her spine and her heartbeat quickened. She wondered if he was an omen to warn her of darker things.

Chapter Two

Brianna swallowed over the hard lump in her throat and shifted on her seat as they slowly drove through the gates. She had yet to decide whether they were gates into heaven or hell. After the man's appearance, she worried they were the latter.

Her hand shook as she lifted it to play with the small golden dragon pendent her mother had given her when she was twelve, fingers sliding over the blue sapphire gem resting in the dragon's claws, trying to push the sense of foreboding the man had elicited in her from her mind as she turned to take in the school grounds.

Her eyes widened as her mouth opened. The trees lining the drive ended to reveal a thick, green expanse of lawn rolling up to a massive, French chateau-style mansion. Brianna sucked in a breath as the scent of roses filled the car. Birds twittered happily as she studied the structure in front of her. The pictures in the brochure had not prepared her for this. If anything, they downplayed the luxury.

"Is this really the school?" She breathed as the nervous energy she had kept inside bubbled to the surface.

Her mother smiled, her eyes taking on a faraway look as she patted her hand. "Yes," she breathed. "It's beautiful, isn't it?"

Brianna nodded. She took in the entry boasting arched passageways from the steps to the heavy wooden doors showcasing ornate carvings of Medusa's head. Two massive wings jutted out from each side of the main entrance. Each had a railed porch where students lounged at tables or did schoolwork.

Brianna tore her eyes away from the building as her mother parked in the cobblestone, circular drive at the base of the steps next to a fountain. Statues of mermaids surrounded the center, water bursting up between them to fall into the shimmering pool beneath.

Before she could reach for her door handle, a man dressed in a tweed suit opened it. His salt and pepper hair combed away from his face and sparkling blue eyes made him quite handsome. Brianna smiled shyly at him as she stood from the car.

"Hello, Samuel," her mother said affectionately as she brushed her pale blonde hair from her face.

"Julie," the man said in a thick Irish accent, giving her a wistful smile that made Brianna shift uncomfortably. "You are as enchanting as ever." He turned back to Brianna, offering his hand. "I'm Samuel Hughes, your guidance counselor. I will be helping you through your transition into our school."

"It's nice to meet you, Mr. Hughes," she said, taking his offered hand and shaking it firmly.

"Call me Sam." His eyes crinkled around the edges as he grinned. "There is no need for formalities here."

Brianna's smile widened. His obvious affection toward her mother aside. She liked him. "It's nice to meet you, Sam. I see you know my mother."

"We've been friends since we were teenagers," her mother said quickly. Brianna narrowed her eyes, realizing that though Sam had an obvious crush on her mother, she only thought of him as a friend. Brianna winced, caught between sympathy for Sam and the discomfort of someone having a crush on her mother.

He gave a short nod, tilting his head toward a small man in a gray suit standing beside one of the front doors. "Norris will get your bags." The man jumped into action at the sound of his name.

Sam swept his arm toward the door and smiled, his welcoming demeanor relaxing her. "Shall we?"

As she took her first step onto the porch, she saw a boy leaning against the wall. He had hair so blond it was almost white, ice-blue eyes and a face so handsome she wondered if she should look away but couldn't. He inclined his head toward her, his expression as hard as stone. His coldness shot straight into her soul, making her shiver, but something else pulled her toward him. She took an unconscious step in his direction.

"Goddess," he said, but the word seemed far from an endearment, causing her to blink and take a step back. There was so much contempt in his face it made her want to seek the comfort of their car again and drive far away.

"Gabriel," Sam snapped, his face losing all kindness, "Get to class."

Gabriel smiled, flashing perfect white teeth. "Don't get your knickers in a twist, Sam," he said, an English accent threading through his words. "I was simply greeting a fellow student. We have to welcome the new arrivals, don't we?"

"Gabriel," Sam narrowed his eyes as the two glared at each other, an unspoken message passing between them. "You can greet her later. I'm sure your instructor has noticed your absence."

Gabriel raised his hands, his face relaxing in false innocence. He glanced toward her mother, who straightened. Brianna frowned. Did her mother know Gabriel?

Gabriel chuckled. "We wouldn't want that, would we? Don't worry. My education will not suffer any longer. I'm going to class, Counselor."

He turned back to Brianna, tilting his head toward her, the contempt returning to his face. "Goddess." He turned to walk into the building.

"Why does he keep calling me that?" Brianna demanded.

Gabriel's back stiffened before he turned toward Sam, then looked at her. All the contempt faded from his face as his curious eyes swept over her again. "She doesn't know?"

Sam gritted his teeth but did not answer. Brianna turned toward her mother, but her stoic face revealed nothing. She glanced toward Gabriel, hoping that he would give her some sort of answer.

He just shook his head, turned on his heel and walked away, leaving her with more questions than answers.

THE INTERIOR OF THE mansion was as opulent as the outside. A large, crystal chandelier dangled over the entryway, casting rays of light upon the marble tiles of the floor. A common area sat to the left, students sitting on fluffy couches and conversing or watching the huge television affixed to one wall. Two massive, curving staircases reached up to the second floor. Heavy wooden doors with golden nameplates were lined up beyond the common area as well as on the opposite side of the entryway. It was to one of these doors Sam led Brianna and her mother, ushering them inside.

He gestured for them to sit in front of his large, oak desk, which sat before floor-to-ceiling bookshelves. Before she sat, Brianna slowly caressed the leather of the high-backed chair that seemed as if it should be displayed in a castle in the British Isles.

"I have your schedule," he began, shuffling through papers on his desk and avoiding Brianna's gaze. She knew why, too. He didn't want her to ask about the conversation with Gabriel, but she was determined not to allow him to get away with keeping secrets.

"What did Gabriel mean?" Brianna asked, crossing her arms over her chest and glancing from Sam to her mother, "I feel like you haven't told me something, something important."

Her mother shifted before sighing, her face tensing as it always did whenever she had been caught in a lie. It hadn't happened often during Brianna's lifetime, which made each instance memorable. "The truth is, Brianna, you *are* here to start new. I didn't lie about that." She rolled her shoulders and straightened her spine before continuing. "However, as one of the alumni's children, your scholarship has been active since your birth. I wasn't going to bring you here until what happened at the fraternity."

Brianna's lip curled as annoyance slid through her at her mother's reasons for not telling her the truth. She didn't want Brianna to put up a fight.

"So much for being special," she said through clenched teeth as she hugged her arms closer to her chest. She looked between her mother and Sam. "I guess everyone here knows what happened then?"

The silence stretched. Brianna narrowed her eyes at Sam, who was glancing at his feet, his cheeks red, no longer charmed by him. "I guess that tells me." She hissed, shaking her head as her fingertips caressed the necklace as if it would protect her from the pain of being lied to.

She looked at her mother. "How is this going to be any different than my old school? Everyone is still going to see me and think, there's the freak who fought off a group of maniacs bent on killing people."

"How did you fight them off, Brianna? You haven't told me much about what happened that night." Her mother raised her brow.

Brianna pressed her lips together. It wasn't that she didn't want to tell her. But how could she tell her that the ones she fought weren't human? That she was the only one who saw what they really were? That a huge surge of energy had wrapped around her, causing her to glow? That she heard a male's voice in her head telling her exactly where to hit?

She couldn't tell her mother any of that. She would think she was crazy.

Her mother sighed. "If you're not going to tell me, I must protect you the best way I can. Here you *will* be protected, and you will find out things you need to know that can help you."

"Why can't you tell me?" Brianna's eyes flashed as her gaze swept over her mother's face.

"I suspect for the same reason you won't tell me what happened," she said, rising from her chair. "You won't believe me."

Brianna swallowed as she stood slowly, realizing her mother was leaving. She struggled not to allow the panic of being left alone to show in her expression.

I'll see you this weekend," her mother said softly, then, turned to Sam, her forehead creasing in worry. "Keep her safe."

Sam nodded as her mother bent kissing her forehead, then, she walked out the door. Only her jasmine scent remained behind. She turned to Sam, the only person who knew what her mother had meant. Unfortunately, she knew he would never tell her.

Chapter Three

An awkward silence stretched between Brianna and Sam until a loud knock on the door made her jump.

"Don't worry," he assured her, giving her a small smile as he strolled to the door. "It's just the student who will be your guide to your first class."

He opened the door, ushering in a girl around Brianna's age dressed in the same school uniform she wore. Her long, chestnut hair was perfectly styled in a sleek ponytail, her make-up was flawless. Her brown eyes sparkled as a smile slid over her pretty face.

"I'm Rowan Walsh," she said, her voice soft as her eyes swept over Brianna, appraising her, just as she knew everyone would be doing. She forced herself not to fidget, showing no weakness for the girl to pick apart.

"It's nice to meet you." Brianna forced a smile. When Sam stepped beside her, she refused to acknowledge him. The truth was, she was still mad at him for helping her mother mislead her. In her mind, he was no longer trustworthy.

"From what I've seen, you will fit in well here," Rowan said, waving her toward the door with a sweep of her small, delicate hand. She took a step before Sam stopped her.

"Brianna, if you need anything, just ask," he said, his deep voice low and guilt-ridden.

She turned to face him. "I'll be fine." Her voice betrayed her anger as she held her chin high.

Sam nodded as he handed her a piece of paper. "Your schedule," he explained. "Greer Newton will be your guide for the rest of your school day. She is also your roommate, so she will show you to your dorm room. She'll meet you after your first class."

Brianna nodded without saying another word and followed Rowen out of the room, forcing a smile over her tight expression.

As soon as they were alone, Rowen turned to her, her lips curling into a sneer. "Did he say Greer was your roommate?"

"Yes," Brianna mumbled, frowning at her schedule. Most classes were subjects she was used to, such as algebra, English, science, and history. Then she had theater, which was her elective, self-defense PE and Latin. However, there was one class that made her frown. Mythological studies. Her thoughts drifted back to Medusa's head emblazoned on her uniform jacket as well as the doors to the school. She shrugged. Maybe it was a special course.

Realizing Rowan was talking, she blinked and looked up from the paper.

"I wouldn't want to room with Greer."

Brianna frowned, taking in Rowen's face, twisted in an expression of disgust and the way she said Greer's name like a curse. "Why?"

"She's...weird," she said, shaking her head then, smiled, a viciousness in it that sent a chill down Brianna's spine. "You'll see."

In all her almost seventeen years, she had always hated bullies, avoiding them at all costs, and Rowan was quickly proving to be one.

She opened her mouth to reply, but her eyes moved over Rowan's shoulder, landing on Gabriel leaning against one of the curved staircases, erasing any retort she was about to say as she studied him. He had been nothing but rude to her, but there was a pull toward him that she didn't understand. His lean, muscled body relaxed as a thin girl with long, ebony hair pressed her body against him. As she studied them, she realized they were an odd couple. Their movements seemed awkward and lacked affection.

Gabe glanced from the girl to Brianna. His lips lifted in a sneer as he inclined his head. "Goddess."

"I'm not willing to deal with your shit today, Gabe," Rowan said before Brianna could speak, rolling her eyes, "So, if you are about to be an ass, do us all a favor and slink back into whatever cave you came out of."

"Aren't you only supposed to bitch and moan at night?" Gabe asked, quirking his brow, his ice-cold eyes sweeping over her.

Rowan's expression was venomous, but instead of answering him, she turned to Brianna. "Come on," she gritted through clenched teeth as she grabbed her arm, her nails digging into her skin as she led her up the stairs. Gabriel and the girl who was now clinging to him laughed. The girl mocked the nickname Gabriel had given her in a nasal voice.

"I don't know why he keeps calling me that," Brianna said, mystified.

Rowan blinked as if she had been slapped. She opened her mouth before closing it, but she quickly recovered her smile. "Don't worry about Gabe or his girlfriend, Neva," she said, shaking her head. "They like to get under people's skin."

"Why do they have to get under mine? I just got here." Brianna frowned, her lips pressing into a hard, thin line.

"That's simply how my brother is."

The voice that had spoken had a pleasant English accent. Brianna jumped and spun, facing a boy as handsome as his brother, yet lacking the coldness in his expression. His hair was brown, and his eyes were a deep amber. His chiseled, flawless face looked almost statue-like. He possessed a strong, muscular body that stood a head over her short frame. A lazy smile stretched across his face.

"I'm Aidan Brandt," he said, his gaze sweeping over her in open appreciation, causing her to blush.

"G-Gabriel is your brother?" Brianna asked, frowning as she searched for any resemblance, finding only a slight likeness in the sharp features that would reveal any relation between them.

"Half-brother...We share the same mother," he said, his lips twitching. "Hence the reason his last name is Isolde."

Brianna blinked. Even his last name made her want to take a step closer to him, even though he had only shown her reasons to run away. It puzzled her that she did not have the same reaction to Aidan.

"You haven't told me your name." He raised his brow, his teeth sliding over his bottom lip.

"Brianna...Brianna Powers."

He nodded and pursed his lips, as if he had known but just needed confirmation.

"It's nice to meet you, Brianna. I hope my brother hasn't ruined your impression of the rest of us."

"He hasn't," she assured him and turned to Rowan, feeling the definite shift in the air as he strolled past them and into the room.

Rowan's expression tightened and her cheeks flushed red, making Brianna wince because she recognized that expression. She had seen it many times before.

Rowan leaned close to Brianna's ear, her floral scent wrapping around her like a snake as Aidan took a seat in the back of the classroom. "If you want to stay in my good graces, you will stay away from Aidan."

Brianna winced again as Rowan brushed past her and into the classroom. Any kindness she had shown her before was gone.

Sighing, she glanced at her schedule, making sure she was in the right place, and walked inside the room. Rowan walked up to a group standing in the corner, immediately whispering to them. They all looked at her with narrowed eyes. Her heart clenched. She had been at the school for less than two hours and had somehow gained the ire of several people.

She straightened her back and turned toward the teacher's desk at the front of the classroom, determined to push it from her mind.

A petite lady with gray hair pulled back in a bun smiled as she reached her hand forward. "You must be Brianna Powers," she said, warmly encasing Brianna's hand in her own. "I'm Mrs. Knight. Welcome to Silver Grove Academy."

"Thank you," Brianna whispered. When she turned and caught Rowan's hateful glare, she was reminded of how unwelcome she felt.

BRIANNA STOOD BY THE door after class, shifting from one foot to the other, unsure of when the mysterious Greer would meet her. She scanned every person who passed, even though she knew it was useless. She didn't even know what Greer looked like and had only Rowan's comment about Greer being weird to go on.

Aidan came up beside her, the smoky scent of his cologne enveloping her as he leaned against the wall. His eyes roamed over her before raising his brow. "Waiting for someone?" His accent sounded thicker than before. Her stomach clenched. Damn if she had always had a weakness for English accents. Still, his voice didn't intrigue her the way Gabriel's voice had.

She pushed that thought away, wondering why she simply couldn't accept the fact Gabriel hated her for some unknown reason and ignore him for the rest of her stay at Silver Grove Academy.

"Someone named Greer," she answered, frowning as her chest tightened. She was beginning to wonder if the girl had forgotten her.

"Greer," he said, smiling, a flash of affection moving through his gaze. "She's a nice girl."

Brianna swallowed. She hoped so. She didn't think she could handle anyone else not liking her on her first day.

Aidan looked down the hall, his gaze softening. "There she is."

Brianna turned toward a girl, who walked with her books pulled close to her chest. She was pretty with long, reddish brown hair, which curled around her face and eyes the color of burnt wood. The way her shoulders hunched forward probably explained why Rowen had thought she was weird. She was just shy, unlike Rowan, who demanded attention with a mere glance.

"Sorry I'm late," Greer said, managing a nervous smile. Her body stilled and her eyes widened slightly when she noticed Aidan standing beside her before her cheeks tinted a pretty pink.

"It's not a problem," Brianna almost whispered, afraid she would scare her.

"Aidan," she forced her head up, her eyes glancing over him quickly, before lowering them again and staring up at him through long, dark lashes. "Thank you for keeping her company."

He chuckled. "Are you thanking me for talking to a beautiful girl?" he asked, giving her a crooked grin that caused her to inhale sharply as Brianna blushed.

Greer opened her mouth, then closed it again as if trying to figure out a way to respond, but Aidan saved her from it.

"I'll walk you both to class."

Greer barely nodded and turned, making her way down the hall, Brianna walking next to her. She took a deep breath, as if summoning all her courage. "I hope people have been nice to you." She glanced at Brianna; her brow furrowed. To her credit, her eyes stayed on Brianna's face.

"Rowan was with her earlier," Aidan said before Brianna could answer. Judging by the grin on his face, he hadn't realized the animosity Rowan had toward her in class.

Greer visibly jerked at her name. "Oh." Her face fell as they reached the door.

Brianna raised her brow, wondering what their history was.

Aidan smiled as he opened the door for them. As soon as he did, Brianna froze, her eyes widening. Gabriel stood in front of them. His handsome face darkened as his eyes moved from Aidan to Brianna, then back again, eyes narrowing, nostrils flared. The expression was gone a moment later.

"I see you've found the new girl," he said, licking his canine with the tip of his tongue. "You're just like a damn bitch in heat."

"Why do you have to be such an asshole, Gabe?" Aidan growled, through clenched teeth.

"Because the man whore mantel was already taken up by you," Gabriel rolled his eyes.

Brianna's heart clenched as she glanced at Aidan. Was he only being nice to her to sleep with her? She swallowed as Greer wrapped her hand around Brianna's wrist and tugged her past the two brothers and into the room, but not before Brianna heard Gabriel chuckle.

"Guess you'll be wanking off tonight," he jeered.

Brianna fought back tears, wishing she stayed in Georgia, because so far, Silver Grove was proving to be hell.

Chapter Four

Brianna exhaled quietly as all the tension left her body when it was time for lunch. She needed a break. Lunch split the day in half, giving her a reprieve to enjoy that the day was half-way over. At the end of the day, she planned on hiding in her room from everyone bent on torturing her.

She paused after she stepped into the cafeteria with Greer at her side, her eyes widening. It wasn't like a regular school cafeteria. In fact, it looked like a restaurant, with white linen-covered tables of varying sizes decorating the room. Each table had silverware wrapped in white cloth napkins and a menu sitting in the middle. Servers scurried from table to table, taking orders. The rich scent of bread coated the air, making Brianna's stomach rumble.

"It's not what you expected, is it?" Greer asked, giving her a wide smile. Her shyness had faded, and Brianna was starting to relax, relieved that someone in this school seemed to like her.

"It's definitely different from my last school in Georgia," Brianna breathed out as she continued to look around in awe, wondering where she should sit.

"Come on," Greer nudged her with her shoulder and led her to a table near the back of the cafeteria. "My friends will join us soon."

Brianna sank into a padded white chair and peered at the girl across from her, the weight in her chest lifting even more. "Greer," Greer looked up from the menu, her brows quirking. "Thank you for being nice to me."

Greer frowned, a shadow moving over her face. She swallowed before she spoke. "I guess people haven't been kind, have they?" she winced. "I mean...I witnessed what happened with Gabe and Aidan."

Brianna shrugged, trying to let the two brothers fade into the dark recesses of her mind. "It's not just them." She pursed her lips. "Rowan threatened me. She told me to stay away from Aidan. Then she and her friends glared at me throughout the entire class. It's safe to say they all hate me."

"That sounds like Rowan." She nodded, then rolled her eyes. "She acts like that to everyone...even her friends."

Brianna sighed. At least she wasn't singled out. "So, she's the mean girl of the school?"

"The meanest...Well, except for Gabe's girlfriend, Neva." She winced as she leaned forward and lowered her voice. "That girl has issues."

"I'm on both of their radars at the moment," Brianna mumbled, sinking further into her chair, suddenly more depressed than before as every bit of the stress that had faded returned.

"Whose radars?" A boy with sable hair that fell over his umber tinted eyes asked as he approached the table. He was cute in a boyish way with a wide grin. Brianna lowered her eyes to his black shirt, the band name *TX2* across the chest.

Beside him stood a tall, slim boy with a crooked grin, dimples popping out on his cheeks. His hair was also a rich sable but cut close to his head. His dark eyes were almost black and sparkled with mischief.

"Rowan and Neva's," Greer gave Brianna a sympathetic smile. "Brianna here gained their hate before the first two classes were over."

"Talented," the boy with the *TX2* t-shirt said, causing Brianna to laugh. The weight in her chest lifted again, and the boy patted her shoulder. "It took me a whole day before they hated the sight of me. But it's their loss because I'm hot."

He ran his hand down his chest before striking a pose that most male models used on the cover of a magazine.

"Skyler..." Greer moaned, rolling her eyes as she giggled.

"Don't deny it." He grinned as he took a seat beside her and draped an arm around her shoulders. "You know you've had naughty dreams about me."

The boy with dimples made a gagging sound and sat beside Brianna, turning to her. "I'm Boyd, by the way."

"Brianna," she smiled.

"In all seriousness, Rowan isn't *that* bad." A frown crossed Boyd's brow as his dark eyes glided over each of them.

"You think that because you want to play doctor with her," Skyler said, chuckling when Boyd's face turned red. "Come to think of it, you want to play doctor with half the girls in this school."

Their joking stopped abruptly as a pretty girl with champagne blonde hair bounced over to their table. Her cobalt blue eyes sparkled as she straightened her perfectly straight skirt. She smiled widely as her eyes fell on Brianna.

"You must be the new girl," she chirped. "I just wanted to introduce myself. I'm Alona Cristoff. I'm the class president."

"It's nice to meet you," Brianna said.

If it were possible, the corner of the girl's lips lifted even more. "If you need anything, let me know." Brianna nodded before Alona bounced away.

"I see she's campaigning again," Greer groaned as her gaze followed Alona, skipping to another table.

"She seemed nice," Brianna stated, frowning as she glanced from Alona to Greer.

Greer shook her head. "Don't get used to it," she warned, meeting Brianna's gaze. "She may be your next enemy."

Brianna's stomach churned. "Why...Why do you say that?"

"She's Aidan's ex." She shifted in her chair, looking over her shoulder at Alona flitting from one table to the next. "They broke up two weeks ago, and she's far from over him."

Brianna sighed, covering her face with her hands. "Great."

Skyler reached across the table and patted her shoulder. "It's okay, Brianna." His smile widened as she glanced at him. "We'll protect you."

She shook her head and sighed, feeling her heart sink. With the way she was amassing enemies, she feared no one could protect her from her new school.

BRIANNA HAD MANAGED to avoid her newfound enemies for the rest of the school day. She ate dinner with Greer, Skyler and Boyd, then Greer led her to a large, white, three-story building behind the school surrounded by other buildings of a similar structure.

"This is our dorm," Greer said, pointing to the name carved into the concrete above the door. Brianna narrowed her eyes as she read.

"Olympus...Really?" she asked as Gabriel's insistence on calling her goddess drifted through her mind, causing her to grit her teeth.

"They are named after mythical places," Greer shrugged, giving her a sunny smile. "Our housemother is Mrs. Galatas. You'll like her. She's nice."

As they stepped into the building, Greer waved at two muscular men at the security station. "She's the new girl," she said, jerking her thumb over her shoulder at Brianna. "Brianna Powers."

"I've signed you both in, Greer," one of the men said, giving her an affectionate wave.

Greer nodded her thanks, then led Brianna to the top floor. She stopped at the room at the far end of the hall and inserted the key, opening the door. When they stepped inside, Brianna glanced around, finding her bed already made, her clothes hanging inside the closet. Two large desks sat beneath the windows on the far wall.

Greer's side of the room was decorated with posters representing different computer games and retro bands from the eighties. A blood-red comforter decorated her bed.

Brianna's side was devoid of any decoration except for her favorite pillow and the blue comforter she had used since she was small on the bed.

"You can decorate your side any way you want," Greer said, shifting on her feet as she twisted her hands in front of her, as if nervous she wouldn't like the room.

"Thank you," Brianna said and yawned. "But right now, all I want to think about is sleep."

Greer grinned. "I understand." She stretched her arms above her head. "It's been a long day, especially for you. You can have the bathroom first. Towels are in the cabinet."

"Thanks," Brianna said as she yawned again, covering her mouth with her hand. She opened a drawer inside the closet and pulled out her pajamas.

Brianna went through her nightly routine of showering and brushing her hair and teeth before walking to her bed. Greer took her turn in the bathroom.

After fluffing her pillow, she laid down, then shifted, trying to find a comfortable position in the strange bed. She heard the shower come on, then frowned at another sound. A low keening came from just outside the window, growing louder and louder.

She sat up and glanced toward it, frowning as a blue light illuminated the room. The glass in the windows visibly shivered, causing her heart to jump in her chest before bursting inward, spraying glass. She covered her head and face with her arms. Once the sound of tinkling glass ended, she lowered her arms, panting.

Her eyes widened as the light brightened, revealing a horrid, screaming woman moving through the window and turning toward her, screeching, with her hands curled. Claws jutted from each fingertip sharp enough to rip through skin.

A scream burst from Brianna's throat as she scrambled up to stand on her bed and backed toward the wall. Her body shimmered as light lit her skin in the same way it had when she had fought the frat boys. This time, though, she was frozen to the spot and there was no voice telling her what to do.

The bathroom door swung open. Greer stepped into the room, a towel wrapped around her hair, dripping wet. She raised her hand, a light shined from it.

"Auferte!" she shouted. The light shot from her, hitting the screaming woman in the chest, and throwing her back out the window.

Greer tiptoed over glass shards, being careful not to cut herself, and thrust her head out the window, her eyes narrowed. "Rowan," she groaned. "That stupid banshee."

Brianna let out a shaky laugh. "Banshee..."

Her head spun. Greer turned toward her, worry masking her face. Brianna knew it was ridiculous, but she had seen it with her own eyes.

Gabriel's comment to Rowan that morning drifted through her mind.

"Aren't you only supposed to bitch and moan at night?"

She blinked, falling to her bed as a shiver slid through her, her mind losing all ability to focus.

Chapter Five

"I told you she needed to be told the truth."

Gabe's concerned voice traveled through her consciousness, the shock of it bringing her back into a world that didn't seem real.

She blinked, lifting her head to glance around, seeing Sam, Greer, Gabriel and a woman she didn't recognize peering at her with concern. She studied each of them, her eyes settling on the stranger. She was gorgeous with long, honey blonde hair, crystal blue eyes, and flawless skin.

"Brianna," she said softly, her voice familiar. She struggled to try to remember where she recognized it from. "Are you alright?"

Brianna blinked, shaking her head. The fear of what she witnessed snaked through her causing her lips to tremble. "T-There was a woman who tried to attack me but..."

Her eyes glided to Greer. What she had seen couldn't have been real. Greer gave her a gentle smile. "I fought her off with glowing hands and a spell?"

Brianna blinked and nodded, waiting for the others to call her and Greer insane, but the accusation never came. Glass from the window sparkled on the floor, broken...like her.

"Goddess," Gabriel said, snapping her back to reality. This time when he said his nickname for her, it lacked the animosity from before. Instead, his voice was filled with affection she never expected he could have for her.

She frowned. "Why do you keep calling me that?"

She bit her lower lip to keep it from trembling as he shrugged. "Because that's what you are. A goddess...The granddaughter of Aphrodite and Ares as well as Hades and Persephone. Daughter of Death and Juliette."

Brianna sat up. "My father is Larry Powers." She snorted. "He's certainly not death. He's an accountant."

"No. He's the man who raised you." Sam said. "He couldn't give your mother children, not that she wanted them from him, so Hades' son, Death, took on that role. He's the biological father of both you and your sister, Sadie." He shifted from foot to foot and looked away, almost as if there was something he wasn't telling her.

Brianna began to laugh hysterically, holding her stomach. This had to be an elaborate prank. It had to be. "You expect me to believe Hades and Persephone are real...That Ares and Aphrodite are real?"

"Well, I hope we're real," the beautiful lady said with a smile, stopping Brianna's laughter because for some reason it made sense that she was exactly who she said she was...A Greek goddess. If Brianna had to guess, she was Aphrodite, the Greek goddess of love and beauty and then, there was her voice...So familiar that she was positive she had heard her speak before. "It would be most inconvenient if I wasn't."

Brianna studied the woman's face, her eyes widening. She could definitely see resemblances between Aphrodite and her mother, then she gasped. She remembered exactly why the voice was so familiar. It was the voice in her head the night the frat boys had attacked. She had told her to sleep.

"You're Aphrodite," Brianna said, her voice hollow, but she knew what she spoke was the truth. "The Goddess of Love. You've spoken to me before."

The woman before her nodded. "Yes, I am Aphrodite, though most call me Mrs. Galatas here," she said, raising her brow. "It helps keep my identity secret, and yes, I spoke to you. It was my way of protecting you when your gifts made themselves known."

"So that makes me—"

"A goddess," Gabriel finished, pushing away from the door he had been lounging against. Brianna frowned. His presence didn't make sense.

"Why are you here?" she asked, shaking her head as she tried to wade through her confusion and fear. She threw up her hands. "Don't you hate me?"

Gabriel's ice-blue eyes flashed. For a moment, she wondered if she had hurt his feelings. "I would leave, but it's in my best interest to keep you safe."

"Dick," Greer muttered, slanting her eyes at him.

"Why thank you, Love. I do have a big one." He smirked. "You want to see it?"

Greer rolled her eyes and turned back to Brianna, her voice softening. "Listen...I realize you don't know me, but I *am* your friend. I never lied about that." She reached forward to clasp Brianna's hands. "I promise this is all true. You *are* a goddess. That's why your skin glows when you fight. I'm sure your grandfather, Ares, gives you instructions. There's a man who speaks to you when you are in danger now, right? In the same way Aphrodite spoke to you?"

Brianna nodded as tears filled her eyes. "Before her, but on the same night. When I fought the fraternity guys, he told me what to do."

"I'm sure you have some gifts from Aphrodite and Death, as well as Hades and Persephone, too," Greer said, softly, "And also your mother."

"Is everyone here a god or goddess?" Brianna asked, a shiver running through her as she realized how ridiculous this conversation sounded. But it wasn't ridiculous, was it? She had witnessed it all. "Are you?"

Greer's hand tightened around hers. "I am the granddaughter of Hecate and Aeetes," she said, her chin rising. "I am a demi-goddess with the option of becoming a goddess in the future, but I'm also a witch. However, I do get my gifts from Hecate, who is the goddess of witchcraft."

"What about him?" Brianna asked, tilting her chin toward Gabriel.

His laughter echoed through the room. "I look like a god, don't I?" His lips tilted into a devilish smirk. "But no. I'm an ice dragon shifter, which is much better in my book."

Brianna swallowed as she turned to Sam. "And you?"

"The grandson of the Oracle," he said, pressing his lips together when Gabriel snorted in disgust.

"What was that...*thing* that came for me tonight?" Brianna asked, trembling when she remembered the ghastly woman with curled claws.

"Rowan," Greer said, rolling her eyes. Brianna's mouth dropped open because she remembered Greer saying that it was Rowan after throwing the glowing, magic ball into her and pushing her out the window but that thing did not look like the perfectly put together Rowan, but Greer continued, stopping Brianna from voicing her doubt. "I worried she may do something after she saw Aidan showing you attention. I didn't think she would be stupid enough to do this."

A growl came from Gabe at the mention of his brother. When Brianna glanced at him, something blue flashed beneath his skin. She quickly turned back to Greer, terrified she would see another monster.

"What is she?" Brianna asked even though Greer had already told her, but it was hard to believe.

"A banshee," Gabriel said. When she glanced at him, the blue flash beneath his skin had faded. He shrugged. "I told you she bitched and moaned at night."

"I thought..." Brianna's voice trailed off, her cheeks heating.

"Oh, I know what you thought, Goddess," he said, his grin stretching across his face. "That dirty mind might make me like you better."

Her blush deepened, but she was relieved that her senses were finally coming back. "What does this mean for me?" she asked, frowning.

Aphrodite cupped her cheek. "It means you're safer here, my beautiful granddaughter, and we will teach you how to defend yourself. This world is much darker for us than mortals, because we are the ones who protect them when they have no idea how close to danger they are. Until you can defend yourself...Until you can fight and even after, we will protect you."

Tears slid down Brianna's cheeks as she thought of her mother. Anger trembled through her because she hadn't told her, hadn't prepared her. She had kept her real father's identity a secret and allowed her to believe a man who barely noticed she was there was her father. Now, she was confused about who she was and what she was meant to do in this world.

"YOU KNOW YOU CAN SKIP class today," Greer said the next morning. Light glowed through the window Aphrodite had fixed with a wave of her hand. "No one would blame you."

Brianna shook her head, her golden blonde ponytail swinging as she smoothed her hands down the blue skirt of her uniform. "I've got to get used to my life now, and hiding in this room is not going to help."

Greer nodded, her features softening as she twisted a lock of her curly, reddish-brown hair around her finger. "I understand," she said, wincing as she let the curl go allowing it to bounce back into its original form. "I still remember when I found out. It was tough."

Brianna gazed at her, her eyes wide. "How *did* you find out?"

"I was adopted," Greer said, her burnt wood-colored eyes darkening as her voice lowered to almost a whisper. "My biological mother wasn't really one for parenting. My adoptive parents died in a car accident. A few days after their funerals, I received a scholarship here. My aunt and uncle didn't really want me, so they shipped me to Silver Grove without a question of how I received a scholarship to such a prestigious school. When I arrived, Rowan and her friends targeted me because Aidan had been assigned as my guide. I was walking in the courtyard alone at night a week after I started and found myself surrounded by banshees. I ended up hurting one of the girls with the gift I didn't know I possessed. Since then, Rowan has found ways to bully me. She blames me for harming one of her sisters."

"At least you fought back," Brianna said on a sigh, swiping a hand over her eyes. "I just stood there...frozen. Rowan could have hurt me, and I wouldn't have lifted a finger to try to stop her."

Greer raised a brow. "You fought ten monsters your first time. I don't think I could have done that."

Brianna winced, the memory of that night still too fresh but Greer was right. She had fought them. "Thanks, Greer."

"Any time," she said, patting Brianna's shoulder as she stood, picking up her books from the desk. "If you need me today, let me know. We share every class but PE, but I'll walk you there and meet you after."

"You are a good friend, Greer."

"I try," she said, moving toward the door to the room as a smile lifted her lips.

They were quiet as they walked down the stairs and out the door of the dormitory. As soon as she stepped into the noisy courtyard, the acrid scent of smoke assaulted her, drawing her gaze toward a wing in the school that was being renovated. Plastic hung over the windows, making Brianna remember the dream she had the night before she had come to Silver Grove. Teachers and students gathered in the center of the courtyard staring up at the windows, as a large man wearing a black cloak slinked beyond them.

Greer gasped and hugged her books closer to her chest. "Oh no..."

"What?" Brianna asked, frowning as she turned toward her.

"Someone has died," she whispered and glanced around the courtyard searching for anyone who seemed to be missing.

"How do you know?"

Greer's eyes were impossibly wide as she turned toward her. "Because Death himself is here."

Brianna turned quickly and sucked in a breath, taking in the cloaked form of her biological father.

Chapter Six

Though they asked the teachers what happened, none of them would give an answer. The courtyard was chaotic. Mrs. Knight was ushering the students to class while Norris rushed from his usual spot beside the door to the abandoned wing to assist Death in any way he asked. Brianna tried to ignore that he grew wings to do this. Students were staring at the building where the tragedy had taken place. Most were worried, but a few joked trying to dispel their fear. Sam approached them, rubbing his fingertips over his furrowed brows.

"The principal wants everyone to get to their classes so they can find out who is unaccounted for."

"Do you know who it was?" Greer asked, her brown eyes wide with worry as she glanced at the building.

"Not yet," he said, his lips pressed into a thin line and his jaw rigid as he gazed upward into nothing.

Greer frowned, trying to understand what had happened. She raised her eyes to the cloaked figure gliding around the abandoned wing before traveling back to Sam. "But Death..."

Sam blinked as Greer gained his attention again. "Is there, but the soul is not." He pinched the bridge of his nose and shook his head as if trying to make sense of it all.

"How is that possible?" Greer asked. Several students stopped chatting to glance at her with puzzled expressions, hoping Sam would give some answers.

Sam ran his shaky hand through his salt-and-pepper hair, causing it to stick up in all directions before his blue eyes traveled from Brianna to Greer. "We're not sure." he said, putting his hand up when she opened her mouth to ask more questions. "The best thing you can do is get to class. After we find out who is missing, maybe I will have more answers."

Greer nodded as Sam walked away, his face pale and his steps slow. No matter how mad she had been at him before, Brianna could see he cared about each student.

She stared after him with her mouth agape, her eyes narrowing as she took in their surroundings again, hoping to find an answer that simply wasn't there.

"Has this ever happened before?" Brianna asked, her heart thumping in her chest. Death was bad, but somehow, she knew a missing soul was worse.

"Not to my knowledge," Greer said, her expression troubled. "But he's right. The sooner we get to class, the sooner they can discover who's missing. It's the only thing we can do to help. Come on. I'll walk with you to the gym."

Brianna followed, glancing over her shoulder at the building. Her eyes widened as the man who she had seen the day before walking along the fence appeared before a door near the end of the hall, but she blinked, and he was gone. She swallowed because that omen brought another to mind. The nightmare of the boy burned beyond recognition.

"BOTH THE COACHES, MR. Malor and Mrs. Black, are shifters." Greer explained, the worry still etched across her face.

"So, they're ice dragons, like Gabriel and Aidan?" Brianna asked, pursing her lips as she tried to understand her new surroundings. She didn't miss Greer's blush at the mention of Aidan, making her wonder if she had a crush on him.

"Aidan isn't an ice dragon," Greer said as she led Brianna into one of the largest gyms she had ever seen. She studied the room, her eyes wide as she took it in. Weapons lined the walls as if it were the most common thing in the world.

"But I thought—"

"Since yours truly is an ice dragon that my brother would be one too?" Gabe chuckled behind them; amusement was clear in his voice.

She turned to him; her mouth suddenly dry. He leaned against the wall beside the door, his arms crossed over his muscled chest, his angelic face smirking in a way that caused her heart to leap. It was hard not to notice how handsome he was.

Brianna pushed the thoughts away as he shook his head.

"Nope where I'm cold, he's hot. He's a fire dragon."

"I admit he's definitely hotter than you," Greer said, flashing her teeth in a grin when his lips curled in disgust.

He groaned, rolling his eyes. "Greer, you didn't get your morning pleasure ritual in, did you?" he asked, licking his canine. "You're cranky."

Greer's grin widened, unfazed. "As a matter of fact, I did. What made me cranky was your face ruining the fantasy."

He grabbed his chest as if wounded.

Brianna let out a huff of breath, exasperated at being in his presence and confused further by her need for him to be there. "What are you doing here? Brianna asked, raising her brow.

"Everyone has a partner they work with here," he said, curling his lip as his ice-blue eyes settled on her face. "Unfortunately, you have been paired with me."

"Lovely," she said as she swiped her hand over her forehead in frustration. "Do all the teachers secretly hate me?"

"Or me," he shrugged, but his expression darkened, and she wondered again if she had hurt his feelings. "I'm not too happy about it either, Goddess. You are untrained and I am...Which means a lot of injuries that will be blamed on me."

Brianna clenched her teeth. Of course, he would only care about things that would affect him.

Greer gave her a sympathetic smile. "I have to get to class." She clutched her books close to her chest, reminding Brianna how shy she had seemed at first. Now, she didn't seem that way at all. "But at least they won't be doing workouts today, so that's good."

"That's where you're wrong, Witchlet," Gabriel said, the smirk moving across his face again. "They want her to train immediately. With everything going on, they want her to be able to defend herself. So, though there will be no training in class today, she will have to meet me after classes."

Greer winced, her pert nose wrinkling. "I'm sorry, Brianna." She flicked a narrowed gaze at Gabriel. "But it is for the best."

Brianna nodded, her shoulders slumping forward as Greer turned.

"I'll see you after class," she said, strutting away, leaving her with Gabriel.

She turned to Gabe, unsure of what to say.

"Gabriel Isolde, Brianna Powers, Skyler Sheldon, and Greer Newton, please come to the office." The female voice crackled over the intercom, echoing through the gym.

Brianna turned to Gabriel, his eyes narrowing with worry. Her stomach twisted in warning, telling her whatever she was being summoned to the office for wasn't good.

WHEN THEY REACHED THE office, they found Sam sitting across from a portly man, who gave Gabe and Brianna a tight smile as they walked in. Black hair grew only on the sides of his head, revealing a shiny pink scalp on top. Gabriel's lips lifted in disgust as Greer moved to sit in the chair beside Sam. Scowling, Gabriel leaned against a bookcase, keeping his distance from everyone. When the door opened and Skyler entered, his brows furrowed, Gabriel slid closer to Brianna, surprising her.

"Miss Powers," the portly man said, snapping her attention to him, "I am Mr. Leo, the principal here. I wish my introduction came under different circumstances.

"And what circumstances are those?" Brianna asked, her heart thundering in her chest as she braced herself.

Mr. Leo's gaze moved to each of them, his smile slid off his face to reveal an expression masked in grief. "We've discovered the identity of the one who died last night." He said, straightening in his chair. "I'm sorry to tell you that Boyd Wright has passed away."

Brianna blinked in shock, eyes welling with tears. She didn't know him well, but he had been nice to her. Greer sobbed. Skyler wrapped her in his arms as his own body shook in grief. Brianna tried to fight her tears because she didn't believe she had the right to cry for a boy she'd only talked to twice. But when she blinked, two tears tracked down her cheeks. Gabriel's gaze moved over her face as he shifted closer. The chill from his body wrapped around her, comforting her in a way she didn't understand.

"How did he die?" she asked, trying to fight the sob in her throat. She took a shuddering breath, trying to push her grief away.

Gabriel's brows furrowed, his expression darkening as his eyes slid over her face, and a second later, she was cradled against his chest. He was comforting her as if he liked her...As if he was her friend.

Mr. Leo's eyes darkened as he glanced between them. "I don't think I should—"

"These are his friends," Gabriel said sharply, his body becoming frigid, but still, she didn't move away. The colder he became, the more comforting his embrace. "They have a right to know."

Mr. Leo's voice broke through the sobbing in the room. "Keep your monster contained, boy," he growled. "One of your kind did this...A dragon."

"He froze to death?" Gabriel asked, the muscles in his arms flexing in a way that made Brianna wonder if he would throttle the man if he wasn't holding her.

"No. He was burned," he hissed, staring at Gabe as if he were something abhorrent.

"Then it wasn't me." He narrowed his eyes. "So quit acting as if I am at fault."

The nightmare Brianna had of a boy burnt beyond recognition came back to her and she lifted her head to look at Mr. Leo. "It was in one of the rooms at the end of the hallway, wasn't it?"

Everyone was silent as they stared at her. Sam stepped toward her. "How did you know?" he asked softly.

"The night before I came here. I had a dream." Her voice cracked as her bottom lip trembled. "I thought it was just a dream...An awful nightmare."

"You didn't know," Gabriel growled, his arms tightening around her. "I told these wankers to tell you who you were immediately. They didn't listen."

Mr. Leo shot Gabriel a glare that held so much animosity Brianna winced as she moved closer into his embrace, trying to protect him the way he was protecting her. "Death will want to see you," he said, turning that awful gaze on her, making her jerk. A warning growl fell from Gabriel's lips.

"You mean my biological father?" She said.

A muscle in Mr. Leo's cheek jumped. He nodded once as he rose. "I'll call him." He glanced around the room. "It would be best if this were a private meeting between father and daughter, though I doubt the dragon will leave. You are all excused from class for the next three days. Mr. Isolde, as one of the dragons who is the least suspect of your species, I expect you to do your job and be the guardian you are supposed to be."

Brianna frowned as Gabriel nodded once. Mr. Leo walked out of the room to retrieve the man named Death who had given Brianna and her sister life.

Chapter Seven

Death stared at her, shifting nervously, his expression fearful as his chest rose and fell quickly. His face was pale as he blinked while biting his full lower lip. Brianna would have laughed if she weren't so angry because she never imagined herself capable of scaring someone so formidable. From beneath the hood of his black cloak, eyes the same shade of cerulean as hers swept over her. With a shaky hand, he pushed the hood from his head, revealing wavy, golden blond locks. She narrowed her eyes, taking in their resemblance, and winced.

"Brianna," he said. His deep voice was steady, but she noticed the underlying worry in his tone.

"Death..." She crossed her arms over her chest, her lip curling in the way she had seen Gabriel do often since meeting him the day before. "I hope you didn't expect me to call you daddy."

Gabe's snort echoed through the room. He was the only one who was allowed to stay as a dragon guardian, though she still did not understand exactly what that meant. Death raised his brow at Gabe, who shrugged innocently while trying to fight the amused grin forcing its way over his face.

"Boy, don't forget who I am," he said, narrowing his eyes. "She is my daughter. I'll give her certain concessions because she has every right to be angry, but I don't give a damn about you or your opinions... no matter what prophecy the Oracle spouted to you."

Brianna narrowed her eyes, her gaze shifting between Gabriel and Death. "What prophecy?"

"Fuck," Gabe groaned, running his hand through his hair. "You had to go and mention *that* to her."

Death grinned malevolently, causing a shiver to run down her spine. "You might want to tell her about that, Jack Frost."

Gabe's eyes narrowed on his, but Death turned toward her and shook his head. "That prophecy is between you and him."

"Yet *you* brought it up," Brianna said through clenched teeth. She was tired of people keeping secrets from her.

"Yes, I did," he said, smirking. "So, you can ask him about it later."

"Fucking soul sucker," Gabe mumbled under his breath.

Death ignored him and moved to lean one hip against the desk. "Mr. Leo says you had a dream." He crossed his arms over his chest, but she swore she saw the pride on his face. "As my daughter, you may have gotten my gift of foresight, but it is only with death. I need for you to recount the dream, so I know whether you actually acquired it and if it can help Boyd."

Brianna pressed her lips together, wanting to deny him, but she realized it was dangerous and selfish to keep it to herself. "Fine," she sighed, recanting everything from the dream.

Once finished, Gabe frowned. "It was a girl?"

"Sexist much?" Death asked, rolling his eyes. "Girls can be killers too."

"But she is a fire dragon," he said, frowning. "There are only two in the school."

"Who are they?" Brianna asked, tilting her head as she studied Gabe's face.

"Leah Wells and Alona Cristoff." His face darkened even further as he ran his hand through his almost white hair and cursed.

"Alona...I met her yesterday," Brianna said, shaking her head because she couldn't believe that the perfect, smiling girl could harm anyone. "She was nice to me."

Gabe scoffed. "Alona is not *nice*." Gabe made quotes with his fingers as he spoke.

Death moved to Mr. Leo's desk and picked up a phone. "Alona Cristoff and Leah Wells... Find them."

She raised a brow as she heard the receptionist move from behind her desk. Death set the phone back in the receiver before turning back to Brianna.

"Pay attention to your dreams," he said, his jaw clenching as his eyes flashed in anger at the girl who had taken Boyd's life and had stolen his soul. "It seems that you have some of my reaper powers. If you have more, tell Sam or just call out my name. I will hear you and I will come to you."

Then he was gone.

Gabe rolled his eyes, an amused smile sliding over his face. "You are going to have some serious daddy issues."

Brianna narrowed her gaze at him. "And you are going to tell me about this prophecy."

His smile slid from his face as he clenched his jaw. "Fine. At training, but you're not going to like it."

"You'd better not lie to me," she said, standing and raising her chin defiantly.

He took a deep breath. "You'll find out, Goddess, that I'm the only one who has told you the truth since you got here."

She opened her mouth to reply, but he put out his hand, stopping her. "I'll walk with you to the cafeteria. We'll talk later when you've had something to eat. We might as well practice afterward since we don't have class."

With that, he turned to leave the room, giving her no choice but to follow.

GREER AND SKYLER WEREN'T in the cafeteria when Gabe dropped Brianna off, telling her he needed to meet Neva. She sank into one of the seats, ordering the first thing on the menu, before burying her face in her hands until the food arrived. She tried to push away the emotions threatening to swamp her. On top of the odd, unpleasant feeling she experienced when Gabe walked out of the cafeteria, she was angry with everyone who had lied to her. Then there was Boyd's death and the fact that she had witnessed it in a dream before it happened. All of it left her exhausted. She sighed, trying to convince herself to pick up her fork and eat.

"Rough day?"

Brianna jerked her head up to see Aidan standing at the table.

She blew out a breath. "Only getting rougher.

He was the last person she wanted to see, especially since Gabe had cryptically told her she would discover he was the only one telling her the truth. If true, Aidan had only been nice to her to sleep with her. She narrowed her eyes at him as he sat down across from her, bouncing his knee.

His amber eyes moved over her, darkening when they reached her angry expression. "I'm not the person Gabe says I am," he said, frowning. "I mean, I used to be, but I'm not anymore."

"What changed?" Brianna asked, the sarcasm dripping from her voice as she rolled her eyes. "Me?"

"No." he shrugged. "Me. Alona and I used to date, but I cheated on her the whole time. I realized how much that hurt her, but she wanted me to be this guy who moved her forward. I'm not that person, but she wanted me to be."

"You're saying she used you?" Brianna asked, frowning because there was a semblance of truth in his words. "Why would she be able to use you that way? What makes you so important?"

"My father is an angel on the high council," he said, shifting uncomfortably. "That's huge in the dragon community."

"I thought you were a dragon," she said, raising her brow. "Not an angel."

"I am," he frowned, confused that she didn't understand. Then his eyes widened slightly, remembering she was new to their world. "Angels and fallen aren't supposed to have relations with humans. My mother is a gorgon...now. She's the same monster as Medusa. She was sentenced to become one after Gabe's birth. They forgave her for my birth because my father is an angel on high, and there is more lenience with higher class angels and their partners, even though it is still against the rules, but Gabe's father is a fallen. They didn't forgive that. With her curse, we became dragons. I'm a fire dragon because my father is an angel. Gabe is an ice dragon because his father is a fallen."

"Seems awful to be punished for falling in love," Brianna uttered, her heart clenching.

Aidan snorted. "My mother doesn't fall in love with anyone," he said, shaking his head. "She barely tolerates *us*. She deserved punishment. She cheated on my father with Gabe's father."

Brianna flinched at the loathing in his voice so filled with violence it was like poison to her heart. She couldn't imagine Gabe and Aidan growing up with no one who loved them. Pain pierced her soul as she imagined them as little boys. Aidan flinched, recognizing her sympathy.

"Anyway, I did change," he said, shrugging as if his childhood didn't matter and yet his jaw clenched so hard she was afraid he would break his teeth. "I don't want to be like her. I don't want to be like my father and used to further someone else's life, either."

"I'm sure Gabe doesn't know that," she said, pursing her lips, wishing the brothers were closer. At least they would have each other. "Maybe you should tell him."

"He wouldn't believe me." He fidgeted as he folded his hands and rested them in his lap. "But I hope you do. I really want to know you,

Brianna." He swallowed as he straightened and stood to leave her with her dinner. "We can be friends, right?"

Brianna sighed. She didn't want any more enemies. "Yes, we can, Aidan."

He smiled as he walked away. Watching him, she wondered what he was going to do if Alona turned out to be the one who killed Boyd. Even though they had broken up, she was certain he still cared about her. If it turned out she was a murderer, it would break his heart.

Chapter Eight

As soon as Brianna placed the last bite of food into her mouth, Gabriel strode up to the table, staring down at her. His arms were crossed over his muscled chest, his legs spaced wide apart. His face was slightly red, confusing her because she was used to his pale hue. It made her wonder if he had worked out without her.

"Ready, Goddess?" he asked, his ice-blue eyes narrowed, and a puff of mist moved from between his lips. He inhaled deeply, his face reddening more. His nostrils flared as if smelling something rotten. Frowning, she inhaled, but the only scents she could detect were the familiar buttery aroma of bread and the remnants of the steak and vegetables in front of her.

"I'm not dressed." She glanced down at her uniform, confused. When she looked back up, she shied away at the anger written all over his face as he narrowed his eyes even more.

"There are extra gym clothes in the locker room," he said, gritting his teeth.

She blinked at the sharpness of his words. "Okay…" She hesitantly rose, wondering why he was so upset. He couldn't be angry at her. Before he left, he seemed fine, even friendly. She couldn't think of anything she had done that would put him in such a foul mood.

She followed behind him in silence, his anger palpable as he burst through the gym doors without glancing back. He led her to the locker room, grabbed some extra clothes, threw them at her, and exited without a word.

She frowned as she changed into shorts and a t-shirt, trying to figure out his mood, then joined him in the gym.

He turned to her, his eyes still brewing with rage. "Have you ever fought without Ares' help?" He snapped.

"No..." Brianna shook her head, bewildered by his anger. It was quickly becoming evident that she was, in fact, the target of his ire, but she still didn't understand what she had done to deserve it.

"Then, let's start with learning the soft spots, which are the eyes, nose, throat, and knees." Gabe frowned. "And, of course, the groin."

"I-I thought you were going to tell me the prophecy first," she stuttered, shifting nervously when he narrowed his eyes further, directing so much of his anger toward her, it was suffocating. The mist moving from between his lips became thicker.

"Try to punch me in the eye," he said, ignoring her. When she didn't move, he gritted his teeth, causing the muscles in his jaw to bulge. "*Now*, Goddess. Don't be a waste of my bloody time."

Anger snaked through her as her muscles tightened. She didn't deserve his fury, and she certainly wouldn't allow him to get away with it. She curled her fist and swung, her anger pushing her knuckles into his jaw.

"Why are you being such an asshole?"

He fell backward but immediately jumped to his feet. "That shouldn't be a problem for you, Goddess," he hissed her nickname, rubbing his jaw. With some satisfaction, she noticed a bruise was forming. "After all, you seem to like assholes."

Her brows furrowed as she lowered her hands. "What the hell are you talking about?"

"My brother's stench is all over you," he growled, nostrils flaring as he took a step toward her.

She stared at him, her mouth dropping open. "Seriously? Are you jealous?" She spat out, her face reddening. Her body sparked for a moment, gold light surrounding her before fading.

He started laughing, unfazed by her gift, making her want to punch him again. "Jealous of Aidan showing you attention?" he asked, jaw clenching. "No, I expected that from him."

She crossed her arms over her chest to keep from punching him again. "Then, what is it?"

"It's the fact that, according to a prophecy, *I* am your guardian," he said, raising his chin. "But you are just stupid enough to kill me along with yourself by associating with unsavory company."

She took a step toward him, staring into his eyes. So, the only reason he'd started being nice to her was for a damn prophecy? "Then don't be my guardian." She moved to walk around him and back toward the locker rooms.

He gripped her biceps. "That's not how it works," he growled. She pulled out of his grasp. "It's not a choice."

"For me, it is." Her gaze burned into his. "The only reason you have been nice to me is because of a prophecy. I thought you were becoming my friend. I was wrong."

"You're acting like this because I hurt your feelings?" Gabe asked, rolling his eyes.

"No." Brianna shook her head. "I'm acting like this because I don't need fake friends and I don't need you to guard me." She turned, not wanting him to see her tears, and walked toward the locker room.

"You're wrong about that," he called after her.

She flipped him off over her shoulder as she stomped into the locker room and changed her clothes. When she stepped back into the gym, she was thankful to find Gabe gone.

BRIANNA CROSSED HER arms over her stomach as she stomped across the campus at a quick pace toward her dorm. She was mumbling to herself through trembling lips about what an asshole Gabe was. Tears stung her eyes. She angrily wiped them away with a shaky hand, wondering why Gabe's anger was upsetting her so much. But the truth unsettled her more. As mean as he could be toward her, she was drawn to him. She wanted to be his friend.

"I'm so stupid," she murmured.

The ache in her chest let her know she wanted more than friendship from him. It was insane. From what she knew of him, he could be rude...Except he had comforted her when she found out about Boyd's death.

She shook her head with a groan, hoping to dispel the confusion rolling through her.

She walked with her head down, lost in her thoughts, until an orange glow made her raise her eyes to the hulking monster in front of her. It was at least ten feet tall, scales covering its entire body, massive red and green wings protruded from its back. She slowly raised her head, staring into a mouth of razor-sharp teeth.

Dragon...Brianna took a cautious step back, but she knew she couldn't get far enough away from its fiery nostrils to do any good. The image of Boyd's burned body chose that moment to rise from her memory.

"Good lizard," she whispered.

Narrowing its eyes, it swiped its tail, forcing Brianna to jump. She landed on the ground with a thud and crouched, her eyes widening when she saw the tail reversing direction toward her again. She huffed. The last thing she wanted to do tonight was play a life-and-death game of jump rope.

Jump and roll to the left. Ares' voice whispered through her mind.

As the tail reached her, she jumped, falling to her back and rolled in the direction her grandfather had indicated, but unfortunately, she stood too soon. The end of the dragon's tail whipped out, hitting her in the abdomen and flinging her through the air before crashing into a statue, her head hitting the marble hard before she sank to the ground in a heap.

Her vision blurred as fire burst over her, the heat of it dangerously close to her skin. The scent of sulfur coated the air as another blast of heat erupted over her.

"Brianna!"

Aidan's voice dripping in panic reached her, but she couldn't keep her eyes open. Her eyelids closed as darkness surrounded her, bringing with it the knowledge that she may not wake up.

"WHERE THE FUCK WERE you?" Death growled, the murderous edge to his voice pulling Brianna from the darkness. She fought to open her eyes, clenching her teeth against the throbbing pain working through her head.

"She dismissed me," Gabe said in a quivering, small voice. "I shouldn't have let her."

"No, you shouldn't have," Aidan snarled, causing her heart to ache. She realized he meant to hurt Gabe with each word. "*I* should be her guardian. You're irresponsible and selfish. She would have been killed if it weren't for me."

"You think I don't know you saved her?" Gabe asked, his voice cracking as if he was about to cry. "I bloody well know I screwed up, but I *am* her guardian. That bothers you, doesn't it? I'm the only one who can heal her. You can't do that."

Something pressed against her lips and though she tried to move away, a cool, gentle hand held her head in place. Warm, thick, and metallic-tasting liquid slid down her throat in such a thick stream that it forced her to swallow or choke.

Blood?

The thought repulsed her, but when the headache faded, she couldn't stop. It was addictive, making her feel better, pushing away the pain that had invaded her body.

She reached up and grasped the wrist that pressed against her lips. The coolness of it absorbed into her skin and comforted her further.

Hearing a groan, her eyes popped open, widening when she saw Gabriel's intense gaze staring down at her. He reached up and gently brushed a strand of hair from her eyes with the tips of his fingers. Gone was the anger before, replaced by worry.

"Drink up, Goddess," he said softly, his voice still gritty with the shame of leaving her alone and in danger. His hand slid to the end of her hair and twisted it around his finger. It was an action filled with so much affection she almost convinced herself he didn't just care for her because of a prophecy...a duty forced upon him.

She continued to suck blood from his wrist. He shivered and pulled his bottom lip between his teeth. Finally, he pulled away, and she found herself reaching for him. He clasped his hand in hers. Although she realized she should pull away from him, another part of her wouldn't allow her to.

"Neva isn't going to be happy about this," Aidan mumbled, causing Brianna to shift her gaze to him. She had almost forgotten he was in the room.

"Neva understands my job here," Gabe snapped.

Brianna winced at the harshness of his words that reminded her that she was a job to him. Her fingers twitched, and his hand tightened on hers as if he feared she would pull away.

"Please stop," she whispered, but it might as well have been a scream.

Death moved in front of her, his eyes raking over her. "She's right." His face hardened as he glanced between the brothers. "She doesn't need this from either of you."

Both Aidan and Gabe bowed their heads. Their argument came to a stop, and she found that since she discovered Death's existence, she had never been thankful for his presence until then.

"Thank you," she said, moving into a sitting position while trying to ignore that she had been drinking Gabe's blood moments before. "Who was the dragon that attacked me?" A shiver ran through her, remembering its razor-sharp teeth.

"Alona," Death answered, his voice dark.

Brianna frowned, trying to understand how the sweet girl she had met could show such violence.

"Did she kill Boyd?" Brianna asked.

Death nodded, his features mournful.

"Where is she? I want to ask her why she killed him and attacked me."

"She's missing." A frown marred Death's brow. "She's been missing since this afternoon."

"Were you able to find Leah Wells?" she asked, frowning.

"She's still in school and obviously shaken that one of her kind did this," Death said.

Brianna nodded as she took a shaky breath. "I don't understand anything. Can someone please tell me what's going on?"

"I'll tell you," Gabe said, taking a deep breath. "Before creation, there was darkness. In that darkness lived magical beings who were in control...or so they thought. They didn't realize darkness itself was an entity. A deity...Nyx. They realized there were other gods, too. Until then, they assumed they were gods. After creation, most adapted, but one refused. His name is Kuraim, and he was furious that he was not a god. He wants to rid the universe of gods and goddesses, then enslave humanity. From some things found in her dorm room, it seems that Alona has become one of his followers and she killed Boyd and tried to kill you in his name."

"As the granddaughter of the original gods of Olympus and the daughter of Death and Juliette, you are a goddess, not a demi-god," Aidan said, frowning "Which means you have more celestial blood than most of the students here and therefore, a target."

"Whether you like it or not, you need a guardian," Death said, crossing his arms over his chest. "Did you really send Gabe away?"

She nodded, glancing at Gabe. He shifted on his feet with his head bowed, waiting for more insults and lecturing. "I did," she whispered, refusing to elaborate because she realized it would cause more trouble for him. "I thought I could take care of myself."

"Don't do it again," Death said sternly, but his cerulean eyes flashed with concern. "His blood is the only blood that can heal you." He glared at Gabe, voice lowering dangerously. "Honestly, it's the only reason he's still alive after leaving you defenseless."

"Can't you change that?" Aidan asked, his amber eyes wide with hope. "I would gladly be her guardian."

Gabe's head snapped up to glare at his brother, but Death's voice stopped anything he was about to say.

"No," he said, narrowing his eyes. "The Oracle chooses and once it's spoken in a prophecy, no one can change it." He turned to Gabe. "In all honesty, I was fine with my daughter being guarded by an ice dragon, but it worries me you seem to have inherited your father's impulsiveness. Regardless, you are her guardian." Death's voice lowered to almost a growl. "I usually wouldn't judge you based on your father being a fallen, but tonight made me wonder if I should. So, I'll leave you with this warning. If anything happens to Brianna and her life is taken, yours will follow."

Brianna's heart twisted as Gabriel swallowed and hung his head farther. Though she knew his actions in the gym were uncalled for, she opened her mouth to defend him, but before she could speak, her father faded away.

She squeezed Gabriel's hand in hers as she understood why there was so much animosity in his expression when he first looked at her. Her safety had been put in his hands, and he had to prove he wasn't like his father.

Aidan gritted his teeth. "The Oracle must be crazy to put one such as you, born such as you were, in a position to protect a goddess' life. Brianna will be lucky if she lives through it."

He turned and stomped out of the room, leaving Brianna with the one who would have to use her life to prove himself to everyone around them.

Chapter Nine

An hour later, Brianna walked out of her room in the infirmary. She was surprised she felt as good as she did before her injuries. Neither Aidan nor Death returned, leaving her and Gabe walking in uncomfortable silence. Her emotions were at odds with each other. She wanted to protect him and draw closer to him, but she remained nothing but a pawn in a game...A prize where her life was on the line and whoever saved it would be the victor. Still, her heart squeezed when she looked at him. He was also a pawn. His life rested on the same line as hers...but with more consequences.

As they stepped into the shadowy corridor near the doors, Gabe turned to her, frowning. "Quit looking at me like that, Goddess."

"Like what?" she asked, not realizing she had been staring.

"Like you pity me," he hissed, but raised his chin while he narrowed his eyes. "Pity is for the weak."

Brianna shook her head, suddenly angry as her mind returned to the fact that he had only been nice to her because he was her guardian. "I wasn't pitying you," she said, her teeth grinding. "As a matter of fact, I'm still pissed at you. At least I know why you're using me. At least I can understand now."

She walked past him, but he grabbed her arm and turned her to face him, the anger sliding off his face as his chest hitched. "What do you mean by using you?"

She raised her eyes to his, frowning, because he obviously didn't see it that way. "You're using me, Gabe," she said through her teeth, "If for no other reason than to show everyone you aren't like your father. You're my guardian to further your own reputation, but I understand. I do. I'm not mad at you about that."

His face paled as a sheen of ice formed on his skin. He stepped closer to her, the coolness of his body sinking into hers, causing her to shiver. "Th-That's not true."

Tears rose in her eyes. She didn't understand why the thought of him using her bothered her so much, even if understandable. She didn't lie when she said she wasn't mad about that. Brianna was simply mad at how he had been acting toward her. Still, it hurt to be used. His eyes touched hers, pain washing over his face.

He opened his mouth, but the door opened, the icy breeze washing over them. They turned to see Neva standing at the entrance. Her dark hair whipped around her face from the wind, her expression furious as she looked between them.

"So, Aidan told the truth," She laughed, but it was bitter, wrapping around them as Brianna's heart clenched. Jealousy or not, she didn't want to hurt the girl. "He said you were holding the little goddess' hand. I didn't want to trust him. So, I came here." Her blue eyes traveled to Brianna. "Did you use your grandmother's power on him? I heard she had a reputation for being a whore."

Brianna flinched. Gabe's narrowed eyes settled on his girlfriend. "Don't talk to her like that," he said, gritting his teeth. "She didn't do anything wrong. Neither did I."

"You were close enough," Neva said, looking pointedly at his hand still wrapped around her biceps. Gabe removed his hand from her as if he had been burned. "You still are."

"We were arguing," he said, shaking his head as his jaw clenched. "Why were you talking to Aidan, anyway?"

"He caught me going into my dorm. He thought I needed to know what was going on behind my back."

"And you believed him?" Gabe asked, his body tensing.

"How can I not when the evidence is in front of me?" she asked, nostrils flaring. "I'm not the type of girl who trusts everything I'm told. I'm the type who has to see it with her own eyes. I have and it's over, Gabe."

She turned, running out the door. Gabe took a step toward her, then gripped the front of his hair and let out a growl of frustration.

"Go after her," Brianna said, softly.

"I can't leave you," he said, taking a deep breath as his eyes met hers. She remembered how all the blame for the attack on her landed on him. She wouldn't do that to him again.

"I'll go with you."

He nodded, but his eyes darkened as his shoulders drooped forward. "Thanks."

As they walked across the courtyard, her heart broke for Gabe because she understood what he was giving up if he continued to be her guardian. Even if he gained his reputation...He stood to lose everything else.

BRIANNA TRAILED BEHIND Gabe near a courtyard flanking a set of dorms, her heart twisting as her eyes moved over him. Judging by his stiff shoulders and determined stride, it was obvious he was upset. Brianna's bottom lip trembled as she mentally kicked herself. Of course, he was. Neva was his girlfriend. Still, something forced the jealousy to rise again with a small voice that declared he was supposed to be hers.

Confused, she shook her head and tamped it down, following him as they made their way across the courtyard toward the dorms.

He stopped, almost causing her to slam into his back, and inhaled. Brianna glanced around them, trying to figure out why they had stopped so suddenly. They stood in front of dorms, similar to her own, with the name Mid-Veil carved into the concrete above the door. He frowned as he glanced at the building. His back straightened as he moved close to the corner, putting his finger to his lips as he crept closer.

Cautiously, she followed him. She heard a slight moan, followed by a growl.

"Do you think he knows?" Aidan asked maliciously, sending a warning trickle down Brianna's spine.

"If he hasn't figured out that you and I have been together the whole time, what makes you think he's smart enough to figure it out now?" Neva crowed.

Gabe jerked as if he had been slapped. Anger for him slithered through Brianna, her skin sparking gold before fading.

"And he didn't follow you?" Aidan asked, his voice wrapping around them, causing Brianna's stomach to twist. For some reason, their betrayal of Gabe was hurting her, too.

"He wouldn't leave his precious goddess," she said, giving a throaty, breathless laugh as the sound of lips meeting skin reached them. "You should have seen how heartbroken he looked. It was almost comical. Of course, when he comes back, I must be with him again. Kuraim wouldn't be happy if I didn't have him under my thumb because of that damn prophecy."

"It shouldn't be hard to keep him confused." Aidan groaned again. "It will distract him from Brianna. We'll ruin any hope of polishing that black reputation. It will remain as it is, maybe worse...especially after her death."

Brianna swallowed hard as she realized they were hoping for her death, all while working to ruin Gabe. Neva moaned again.

Gabe straightened as he moved around the corner, arms crossed. "It seems I'm smarter than you thought."

His eyes became even bluer than they normally were, giving an ethereal glow as the tendons stood out on his neck.

Neva's gasp rang out as Aidan swore softly.

"You think I'm a fool?" Gabe hissed. "You are the fools if you are on Kuraim's side. He will eat you whole when he's done with you."

Neva laughed. "Not when he's my father."

"He lied to you," Gabe said with a snarl. "He's not a fallen or a dragon. He can't be your father."

"He's more of a father than that piece of shit fallen who sired me," she snarled. "He was there for me...More than anyone or anything else. He has become my world."

"You've lost your bloody senses, Neva," Gabe said, the pity coating his voice.

She laughed. "I'm more awake now than I've ever been. Kuraim is everything!" Her voice had taken on an obsession that sent chills down Brianna's spine. Hearing a roll of thunder, Brianna glanced at the sky. Lightning burst from it in angry, jagged streaks.

Gabe glanced up, his lips curving into a cold smile. "You should have never betrayed the gods. Ares must have told Zeus of your treachery. My reputation may be black, but yours will be much darker after this."

Aidan laughed, the tone condescending. "Ares only watches Brianna."

"Exactly," Gabe said, nostrils flaring. "You two were stupid enough to think there wasn't a third option. Brianna offered to come with me to talk to you, Neva."

Lightning cracked, hitting a tree in the courtyard, making Brianna jump. Fire rose from the side of the building, the scent of sulfur blanketing the air. Gabe threw himself out of the path, pulling Brianna into the protective shield of his body. Brianna turned her head slightly, seeing two great massive beasts, one red, one blue, rising into the sky, trying to escape the lightning. Brianna's eyes widened at the dragon forms of Aidan and Neva. A roar burst from their mouths. A moment later, a thick black fog curled around them, blocking them from sight. It dissipated quickly, leaving no sign that Aidan and Neva were ever there.

Chapter Ten

Gabe's whole body shook, his dragon flashing beneath his skin, as he continued to stare up at the sky. Brianna gazed at him, entranced by the dragon. Her heart clenched as she experienced his pain. She stepped forward and touched his shoulder. He shrugged it away, causing the pain in her heart to spread through her. Tears sprang to her eyes.

"What did I tell you about pity, Goddess?" He asked through clenched teeth, his body rigid as his muscles tightened beneath his skin.

"It's not pity," she whispered, her voice gritty with heartache. "Was it pity when you embraced me after Boyd's death?"

"No." Another tremor moved through his body. His glowing blue eyes met hers, softening as his dragon ceased its need to be freed. "I saw your friends comforting each other and the pain on your face. I...I just wanted you to feel better...Like someone gave a damn about your feelings."

She stepped in front of him, keeping her eyes on his. She wanted him to see that she cared about him. "That's what I want to do for you," she whispered. His grief-stricken eyes glowed in the dim light around them, roaming over her face as if searching for the truth in her words. "It's not pity, Gabe. I want to be your friend. I want to help you through this."

A tear escaped his eye, freezing on his skin as he released his breath. His body fell against hers, his minty scent enveloped her as he wrapped his arms around her waist. He pulled her close before dropping his head on her shoulder. A sob broke from his throat as teardrop pieces of ice fell on her shirt, melting against her skin. Gabe gripped the fabric of her shirt in the back, as if he were afraid she would disappear, pulling her even closer as his grief engraved into her soul. Her heart broke as she realized he probably never had anyone comfort him the way she was now. If he did, it was from Neva and it had now been proven to be done with a false heart.

She tightened her embrace, pushing the heat of her body into his cold skin, hoping it would heal a piece of his shattered soul.

GABE'S SOBS TORE AT her heart, stopping with an abruptness that left her wondering if he had truly cried out all his grief. He moved away from her with his eyes downcast and his shoulders hunched. They stood in silence for a few moments before he lifted his head and straightened his spine, his usual indifference sliding over his face.

"We need to tell Sam," he said, his wavering voice betraying the worry he tried to hide most of the time. "He's not going to be happy with me again because you were so close to danger when you haven't been trained."

She frowned. "I chose to go. We didn't know there would be any danger. I'll make sure he knows that."

He gave her a small, bitter smile that spoke of years of taking the blame even when the sins committed weren't his own. "It won't matter."

Brianna pursed her lips, determined that he wouldn't take on the guilt for something he couldn't control. "We'll see."

He tilted his head in the direction of the school, then turned and walked toward it with his hands shoved in his pockets and his shoulders bowed forward. She walked quickly, catching up to him.

"Can I ask you something?"

"After what just happened, you can ask anything you want," he said. She wasn't sure whether he was talking about Aidan and Neva's betrayal or comforting him while he cried. Perhaps both.

"Why do the people in the school treat you as if you are like your father?" She asked.

He tensed, the muscles rippling across his back. She could tell he was fighting his temper.

"I'm sorry," she said, shaking her head immediately, regretting upsetting him when he had already been through so much. "I shouldn't have asked."

"No." He swallowed, his body relaxing. "You should have. I mean, you need to know, especially since we'll be around each other a lot."

He shifted, running his hand through his almost white hair, causing it to stick up in every direction. "Children of the fallen often go bad. All of us must fight it. It's in our nature to be rebellious. We all have horrible tempers and act on impulse. Sometimes, we can be dangerous."

"But you *are* fighting it, Gabe. I can see that you are trying."

He stopped walking and turned to her, his features twisting in confusion as his eyes roamed her face.

"Did I say something wrong?"

He continued to rake his gaze over her, an expression that was pained but tender sweeping over his features.

"No," he said, his lip trembling. "No one has ever said that to me."

"Surely someone..."

He shook his head. "No, Brianna." He tilted his head as he studied her, picking her apart. "No one, but I can't blame them. They see the bad in me. It's there. I don't want you to think it's not. I fight it every single day. Fallen lose their ability to care about anyone or anything if they aren't careful. No child of the fallen...No ice dragon has ever been chosen as a guardian. So, I guess you were right earlier when you said I was using you for my reputation, but I'm not doing it to be cruel. As much as I have to prove to them that I'm not evil, I must prove it to myself, too."

"It's not enough for me to believe it?" She asked, frowning. "Maybe I can sway them. After all, I am a goddess."

He smiled sadly. "It comforts me that you want to try, but you're the grandchild of Aphrodite. Sadly, she has a reputation of her own that has been passed down to her children and grandchildren."

"Which is?"

"Finding the admirable qualities in everyone." His face fell. "What you see in me could very well be part of your nature. After all, many only see the temperament of Ares, which runs rather toward the violent side, but Aphrodite will argue he's lovable, protective and kind."

"Does Aphrodite believe you're good?" She gave him a small smile.

He laughed and shook his head. "She's...cautious. But at least she didn't object outright to me being your guardian, like everyone else in this bloody school. She accepted the prophecy. She even calls me her favorite dragon."

"The prophecy..." He blanched as if he had said something wrong. She narrowed her eyes. "Is there anything else in the prophecy?"

He shrugged, hesitant. "The Oracle speaks in riddles," he said, shifting, a shadow falling over his face. "Some of the things she says make little sense, and much of it is misinterpreted."

"Yet you knew you were my guardian from it..." She pointed at him. "You said you would never lie to me."

"I haven't lied to you."

"Lying by omission." She swallowed. "Tell me what she said."

"You're not going to like it." He squinted at her, a muscle in his cheek twitched.

He sighed, looking into the distance. "There were actually two prophecies that foretold your coming and my guardianship. The first was when I first arrived here at the age of twelve on a scholarship from your grandfather, Hades. When he visited Mid-Veil, he noticed that I was different from others of my kind and paid for my schooling. The other beings here weren't convinced. They wanted to make sure I wasn't evil. Only Sam and your family know of the prophecy given at that time. Sam had hoped that it would change by the time of your arrival, but it didn't."

"I'm glad it didn't," she said, her eyes finding his.

"Honestly, I assumed you had been informed that I was your guardian at the age of twelve and was upset you never reached out to me, especially after I gave you that necklace. I assumed it was because I was an ice dragon, and you were trying to reject me." He pointed at the dragon pendant. "It's the symbol of our kind."

Her hand flew to the necklace. "I was told it was a gift from my mother." Anger slithered through her again because her mother had not only kept the secret from her but had hurt Gabe by allowing him to feel as if she rejected him like everyone else. "I guess I should be happy she gave me your gift."

"I suppose so, but it caused a bit of confusion. It's why I treated you so coldly. It wasn't until you arrived that I realized you had never been told who you were, but then I convinced myself you would reject me anyway, so I continued to be rather unpleasant." He winced. "I apologize for being rude."

Brianna grinned. "I would never deny your guardianship based on your lineage but thank you for the apology."

He nodded, his body straightening and his shoulders relaxing. "The second prophecy happened right before your arrival."

"Do both of the prophecies say the same thing?" She asked, frowning.

"Pretty much, but the second one went into more detail."

"Then tell me that one."

He swallowed, then spoke in a monotone voice. "From the darkness and ice comes the guardian of the daughter of Death. Suspect from the first. Only his blood will heal the descendant of love and those who perish. Twin souls of light and night face the one where evil began. The killer of gods where one must stand and one must fall facing betrayals of many. Love conquers all but can destroy. Evil becomes good and good becomes evil. The clash of sharers of blood where Aphrodite's blood cries as one lives and one falls to doom. Only this sacrifice will save them all."

"So...One of us will die?" She asked as a tremble slid through her.

"This is why I didn't want to tell you." he said, running his hand through his hair, frustrated. "The Oracle's words rarely mean what you think they do."

"What if they do?"

Gabe gave her a crooked smile. "Then I will make sure you aren't the one to die, Goddess."

She opened her mouth to tell him she didn't want him to die, either, but something told her it was the last thing he wanted her to say. She straightened as she decided that she needed to find out more and to do that, she needed to find the woman who gave the original prophecies. She had to find the Oracle.

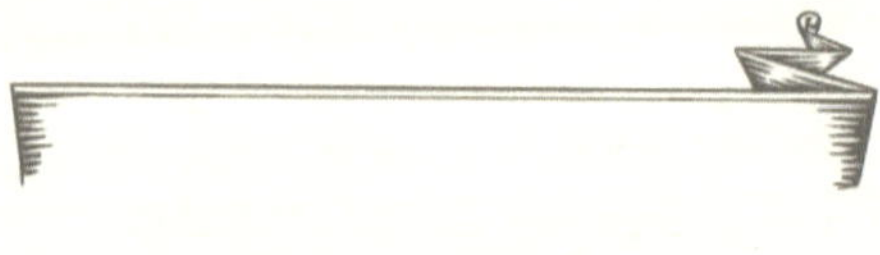

Chapter Eleven

In the apartment on the top floor of the school, Sam paced, muttering to himself. From the couch, Brianna's eyes followed his quick steps. Gabe sat next to her, rubbing his hand over his pale face.

Sam stopped in front of them. "Are you sure?" he asked for the third time since they arrived. He scratched his cheek, peering at them in a way that told Brianna he was hoping to get a different answer.

"I heard it too," Brianna said softly. Did he not trust it because Gabe was the one who said it, or was it because Aidan had never shown anything but loyalty to the school and the gods?

Sam cursed, his hands clenching into fists, then shook his head. "How did we not see this?" He pinched the bridge of his nose. "Are all the dragons involved in this?"

Gabriel bristled, his teeth clenching as he stared up at Sam. "Obviously not, if I'm sitting on your couch trying to protect Brianna."

Sam winced. "I meant the other—"

"I *know* what you meant, Sam." Gabe's eyes narrowed as he rolled his neck and shoulders, trying to release the tightness in his muscles. "But as the Oracle's descendant, you are the guardian of the whole school, whereas I am beholden to Brianna alone."

Brianna pursed her lips, studying him. "As the grandson of the Oracle, why don't you give prophecies?"

Sam winced, shaking his head. "It is my grandmother's job to give prophecies. It won't be passed on to me until after my mother dies."

"How long would that be?" Brianna raised her brow.

He waved his hand absently. "Centuries."

She blinked, gaze raking over him as she tried to guess his age, realizing it was fruitless. Aphrodite appeared to be in her twenties when she was centuries old.

"How old *are* you?"

"Brianna!" Sam chastised, his eyes widening as red bloomed across his cheeks. "We have other things to worry about."

Brianna shrugged, staring at him with wide eyes. "Well, I just wondered if another prophecy might help," she said, shifting closer to Gabe. "I mean...I could go see her, couldn't I?"

"No!" Gabe said sharply, his eyes glowing. "Absolutely not!"

Her mouth dropped open. "Why not?" Brianna asked, crossing her arms over her chest.

"Because you're already worried about what she said last time." Blue flashed beneath his skin. "Her riddles will only make it worse."

She sighed. "But—"

"He's right," Sam said softly. "Grandmother never speaks plainly, and the prophecies often don't mean what you assume they do. We were amazed that part of it was plain enough we understood that Gabriel was your guardian."

She shrugged as she threw up her hands. "Fine." But it wasn't. She was determined to find a way to speak with the Oracle, even if Gabe and Sam didn't want her to.

Gabriel's eyes slid to her, narrowing. "You're looking awfully stubborn over there, Goddess."

Purposely ignoring him, she faced Sam. "Kuraim wants to destroy people like me, right?" Out of the corner of her eyes, she saw Gabe's eyes narrow further. "What about my mother? My sister? She's like me, but she's just as clueless as I was when I came here."

"Sadie hasn't matured into her powers yet. Kuraim won't be able to track her." Sam's voice lowered. "As for Julie...She's always been stubborn. She won't come to the school to stay, but I suppose she will want you to stay here until this is over, especially now that we know who is at fault for Boyd's death."

"I won't get to go home?" Brianna asked, her heart sinking. As crazy as her mother made her, she missed her.

"Don't worry." Gabriel sighed. "I'll keep you company. I'm not going home, either...Not that I really want to."

The troubled expression on his face gripped her heart. "Okay," she whispered, then turned back to Sam. "So, Aidan's obviously teamed up with Kuraim, which means he wants me dead. Why was he so set on being my guardian, then?"

"Because he would be close," Sam said, swallowing as he swiped his hand across his eyes. "He would be able to kill you and steal your soul much easier."

She winced as she realized every moment with him was part of his plan to kill her. "And Boyd's soul is with Kuraim?" Her heart ached at the thought of the boy who would have been her friend, unable to find peace in death. "Why did he want it?"

"To prevent the Gods from returning him to earth." Sam shook his head. "Most of the time, they send the children of gods and goddesses who haven't matured to Hades or Hel or another god or goddess of an underworld to distribute as they please in the afterlife. The explanation I gave you doesn't feel right, but it's the only one I have right now."

"Has Mr. Leo been called?" Brianna asked.

Sam nodded. "And your father."

Brianna huffed. "He's *not* my father."

"Whether you like it or not, Brianna, my blood runs through your veins." She spun to look over her shoulder, seeing Death standing behind her. "That does, in fact, make me your father."

She narrowed her eyes at him, wondering how long he'd been there listening to their conversation. Gabriel stiffened as Death's eyes slid over him with his eyebrow raised, then moved to stand beside Sam.

"Guardian, you did well in protecting her," he said, his face stoic.

Gabriel nodded, but remained silent as Death slid his hood back from his face.

"Aidan's father has been notified, and he's searching for him. He is convinced something else is driving him to do this."

"I witnessed it," Brianna ground out. Why wouldn't they accept the fact that Aidan was evil, yet were more than willing to believe that Gabe was capable of all kinds of dark deeds? "He was a willing participant in it all."

Death tilted his head, his cerulean eyes raking over her face. "I trust you, but he can't comprehend how his son is capable of this."

"He wouldn't have given it a second thought if it had been Gabe," Brianna said, her nostrils flaring.

Death nodded. "You're right. But what Gabriel did tonight has proven a great deal to me. That will have to be enough for you for now."

"You're saying there are still people who don't trust him?" Her hands curled into fists.

"You must remember, the grudge against the fallen is ancient," Death said, rubbing his hand through his hair. "It will take a lot to convince them he isn't who they believe he is. As long as he continues to have a good heart, I'll trust him. I won't lie, though. The fact he's protecting my daughter helps."

She opened her mouth to correct him, but Gabe gripped her hand, squeezing it slightly. She pressed her lips together, deciding she would be silent for him.

"You should get back to the dorm," Death said, glancing out the window behind them at the dark sky. "Gabriel, Sam has given the guards permission to allow you into Brianna's building. A room has been set up next to hers for you. Aphrodite has installed a door between the rooms to be used in case she's in danger. Your possessions have been moved already. Keep her safe." He nodded at Gabe. "I understand now why the Oracle chose you."

Gabriel sucked in a breath, back straightening. Brianna could have sworn he was proud for the first time in his life. She understood how much fulfilling the prophecy meant to him, but she needed reassurance that neither of them would die in the process. She needed to find a way to visit the Oracle.

As the thought drifted through her mind, Death tilted his head, giving her a small smile.

"Brianna, if you want to visit with the Oracle, I will take you tomorrow," he said, raising a brow. "Classes have been canceled. Only your training will commence."

Brianna blinked, realizing he had read her mind. She pressed her lips together as she pushed the annoyance away. After all, she was getting what she wanted. Gabriel stared at her with a furrowed brow. She knew he wanted to protest, but she needed to know if there was a way that both of them would live. Slowly, she nodded.

"Bloody hell," Gabriel groaned, burying his face in his hands. She smiled. Since Death was taking her, neither Sam nor Gabriel could stop her.

Chapter Twelve

Gabriel walked beside Brianna in stony silence, nostrils flaring. As soon as they reached the door of her room, he walked to his, the muscles in his jaw tight. She could tell he was still mad at her because she used her father to gain access to the Oracle.

"Come through the adjoining door if you need me," he said, his voice sharp enough to make her wince. She didn't miss the puff of icy mist that moved from between his lips. Then he walked through the door and closed it behind him.

She stepped inside, seeing Greer sound asleep in her bed, her blood-red blankets pulled up to her head. Brianna's gaze moved to the adjoining door and swallowed. She sighed and walked into the bathroom, preparing for bed.

As she walked out of the bathroom, pulling her hair up in a hair tie, her eyes fell on the adjoining door again. Gabe's cold expression as they walked back to the room entered her mind, gripping it in a way that wouldn't let her go until he was no longer angry at her.

She straightened as she moved toward the door, grasping the knob and turning. She stepped into his room and closed the door behind her, turning...her heart stopping. Gabe stood in the center of the room, shirtless, his almost white hair mussed from pulling the shirt in his hand over his head. Her mouth was suddenly dry as she took in his muscular back. Her eyes widened as he turned, displaying his cut abs and that delicious v that had always been her weakness. She took a shuddering breath. He was absolutely beautiful.

She forced her eyes to his, shifting when he raised a brow, his eyes sparking with heat and causing that odd blue glow to light behind them. "Maybe I should have told you to knock first." His voice was strangely hoarse.

She blushed, realizing she'd been caught ogling him. "I-I'm sorry," she whispered, trying to keep her eyes from roaming over him again.

"Did you want something, Goddess?" He asked as his gaze moved over her. "From what I can see, you are not in any danger." He tossed his shirt in a hamper and took a step toward her.

She swallowed. "I-I wanted to know if you are angry at me," she said, shifting beneath his gaze. "You seemed upset."

He narrowed his eyes. The glow dimmed behind them. "I'm just your guardian, Goddess. My feelings don't matter."

She swallowed over the pain in her heart at his words. "I don't think of you as just my guardian. You're my friend. Your feelings do matter to me."

He raised an eyebrow. "And yet, you ignored my advice not to see the Oracle as soon as your daddy offered to take you," he spat out before pressing his lips together, wincing. He ran his hand through his hair and blew out a breath, mist forming in front of him. His voice softened. "I was trying to protect you and you ignored it."

She tilted her head as his shoulders drooped forward, the muscles in his back rigid. "You're not angry," she whispered, her heart clenching. "I hurt your feelings."

The muscles in his jaw flexed as he turned away from her.

She stepped forward with her hands out. "I'm sorry, Gabe," she whispered, standing in front of him so he couldn't ignore her. "I wanted to help. But if it means that much to you, I'll tell Death I don't want to go."

He turned back to her, a small smile moving across his face, causing her heart to skip a beat as he shook his head. "No, Death will pitch a tantrum like a toddler who just had his candy taken from him if you don't go." His eyes moved over her face. "It's not something I want to deal with."

"Then come with me."

He groaned. "Don't you want daddy-daughter time? Death is perfectly capable of protecting you."

She glared at him. "He is *not* my daddy." She curled her fists at her side, causing Gabe's lips to twitch. "And I don't want to spend time with him, especially alone."

He flashed a grin. "Relax, Goddess. I was going to go with you, anyway." She narrowed her eyes. He was intentionally trying to get a rise out of her. "I have to as your guardian. So, don't worry. The Oracle will be confusing us both."

"Okay," Brianna said, softly, shifting awkwardly. Now that he no longer seemed angry with her, she had no other reason to stay.

She glanced over her shoulder at the door leading to her room. "Well, I guess I'll get back to my room to stare at the ceiling. There is no way I'm going to be able to sleep with everything going through my mind."

"You can stay here and watch a movie." He picked up his laptop from the desk, his lips tugging into a smile.

"Is it allowed?" Brianna asked, chewing her bottom lip.

Gabe shrugged and moved close, his minty scent washing over her. "Not really, but what are they going to do? Kick out the only one who can protect you?" His lips twitched as he leaned forward and whispered into her ear, his cool breath caressing her earlobe. "Live a little, Goddess."

She suppressed a shiver as he walked toward the bed and fluffed the pillows before sitting on top of the covers, leaving plenty of room for her to sit beside him. She grinned and glanced back toward the door, then shook her head. He was right. She needed time to shut off her mind and have fun. She climbed on to the bed, taking the space beside him.

"What are we watching?" She asked.

He chuckled and brought up *The Breakfast Club* hitting play. She leaned against the headboard, settling in beside Gabe as the opening credits moved across the screen.

BRIANNA AWOKE WITH the morning light shining through the window of Gabe's room. Her head lay on his strong chest, his heart beating in the same rhythm as her own beneath her ear. His arm was wrapped around her waist, sending tingles through her body where his hand cupped her hip as he pulled her close against his side in his sleep with his laptop still balanced on his thighs. The minty scent that she always associated with him wrapped around her as a blush settled over her face. She realized at some point in her sleep; she had cuddled close to him.

She raised her head, studying his face as he slept. The muscles in his jaw were relaxed, his features softened, losing some of the sharpness they held in his waking hours. He was sucking his full bottom lip into his mouth, transfixing her, as images of what he must have looked like as a little boy flashed through her mind. Even though people constantly labeled him as a bad seed, she wondered if they would change their minds seeing him like this. While asleep, he appeared almost angelic.

She took a shaky breath as she lifted her eyes, seeing that he was no longer asleep. His eyes were opened roaming her face. A frown marred his brow, making him appear vulnerable as the silence stretched between them.

"You're going to give me a complex if you keep staring at me, Goddess," he said, his lips tilting in a knowing smile. It cast away the appearance of innocence she had witnessed moments before.

She sighed and shook her head, wishing she could hide from him. He had just caught her staring at him again. Her face turned from pink to crimson. "I was afraid to move and wake you. After everything you've gone through, you need the sleep."

His eyes flashed, but his smile stayed in place, covering the pain of Neva and Aidan's betrayal. He tightened his arm around her waist, as if seeking comfort. His fingertips pressed into her hip, preventing her from moving.

"I'm okay, Goddess," he said, brushing a stray strand of hair from her face with the fingertips of his free hand. The action was so tender it sent a pang through her heart.

Her mind drifted to the night before when he had sobbed in her embrace, but she didn't want to bring it up in this quiet moment. Instead, she nodded, deciding to drop it.

His lips twitched as the light flickered in his blue eyes. "You better get back to your room," he said, chuckling, his laughter rumbling through his chest and into her. "I'm sure Death will not like finding you in bed with me, no matter how G-rated it was. Though I have always wondered if Death could die of a coronary. That would definitely put his heart to the test."

She sat up, careful not to jostle the laptop. His arm was still around her waist. Though he seemed hesitant, he slowly released her. The moment he did, her heart tugged in longing. She wanted to stay curled up next to him. She sighed, casting the thought away.

"Let's not push it," she said, shrugging, hoping the action didn't betray her emotions. "Meet me in my room in twenty."

"I'll be there, Goddess." He chuckled again. "I may not knock before I enter. After all, I think it's only fair if I find you shirtless in there."

She rolled her eyes before standing from the bed and moving toward the door, ignoring the heat burning in her cheeks. "Thanks for keeping me company last night."

"You have an open invitation."

She smiled, suddenly shy, and nodded before turning back to the door. She opened it quietly and stepped through, closing it behind her. She stopped suddenly when she found Greer on the other side, her arms crossed over her chest. Her brows raised as she glanced from Brianna to the door with a knowing grin.

"Not a word," Brianna said, raising a finger, wondering how many times she was going to blush that morning. "It was totally innocent."

"I'm not sure innocence and Gabe are allowed in the same sentence," she said, chuckling. "But don't worry. I'm not telling anyone."

"Thanks," Brianna said, shaking her head as she walked toward the bathroom to brush her teeth.

"My silence has a price," Greer called after her. Brianna turned to study her best friend, who was grinning widely.

"Which is?"

"Aphrodite said you're going to see the Oracle." Greer lifted her brows. "Take me with you. I want to hear what she says myself...Just in case I can help."

"You got it," Brianna grinned, walking in the bathroom with thoughts of everything that had happened in her two days at the school running through her mind, but more than that, was the churning in her heart. Though she didn't want to admit it, she knew it was caused by the boy in the next room.

Chapter Thirteen

Death narrowed his eyes when he realized Greer was joining Brianna, Gabe and himself on their journey to the Oracle. His cheeks reddened as he ground his teeth. The scent of sulfur moved through the room as fire flashed in his eyes. She raised her brows at his barely contained temper, waiting for him to explode.

"I had hoped to have time to talk to you *alone*," he said through his teeth, his gaze moving between Brianna and Gabe before settling on her once more.

She smiled sweetly, feeling a certain satisfaction that he was annoyed. "My guardian must go with me for protection so we wouldn't have been alone," she said innocently, barely containing her laughter. "The Oracle has made it clear. He must be at my side at all times."

"I suppose so." Death tilted his head as he studied his daughter. "But Hecate's granddaughter? What is your excuse for her?"

"She's my friend," Brianna shrugged. "I may need her support. Neither of us knows what the Oracle is going to say. It could be...traumatic."

"Fine," he said, his lips twitching into a feral grin that reminded her that she was dealing with a god whose job it was to retrieve souls. "But you *will* speak to me alone when we return."

"Fine." She crossed her arms over her chest. She knew he would never physically harm her, but she could hear the threat of not taking her if she refused in his voice. "But you have to be nice to Gabe and

Greer." She stared at her nails before piercing him with her gaze. "Death knows how to be nice, right?"

Gabe chuckled, but at Death's glare, he turned it into a cough. "Sorry," he said, fighting to keep his lips from twitching into a grin. "Frog in my throat."

Death opened his mouth and then shut it at Brianna's raised brows. He rolled his eyes and lifted his hands in a defensive gesture. Instead of a cutting remark, thick black fog surrounded them.

When the fog cleared, Brianna glanced around a room that reminded her of Sam's apartment, bookshelf after bookshelf crammed with scrolls and books falling from them. The aroma of apples and cinnamon drifted through the room, casting away the previous scent of sulfur.

"This is it?" She asked, frowning as she took in the otherwise normal room while pursing her lips.

"What did you expect, Goddess?" Gabe asked, his lips twitching in amusement. "Tarot cards and crystal balls?"

She pressed her lips together. That was exactly what she thought she would find. Gabe gave a short, amused laugh and shook his head at her obvious ignorance of the world she had been thrust into.

Brianna narrowed her eyes, but her ire ended when a woman made her way through the door and stopped in front of them, her dark brow raised. Hair the color of cherry wood surrounded her head like a halo. She was gorgeous, with blue eyes and tanned skin. A long, flowing dress with bright, vibrant flowers set in a background of black hung over her thin, athletic frame. She appeared young...Too young to be generations older than Sam.

"I thought the Oracle was Sam's grandmother," she whispered to Greer standing beside her as the woman smirked.

"You must let go of your human ideas," Death said, raising a brow. "We age differently here."

"But you and my mother—"

"Work a glamour to make you more comfortable," he said, smiling when she blinked in shock. "In our true forms, we appear only a little older than you. Gods and goddesses, as well as most mythological beings, stop aging in our twenties."

She winced at the image in her mind. She couldn't imagine calling someone who appeared a little older than herself mom.

Gabe grinned. "It takes some getting used to."

"Guardian," she said, addressing Gabe in a rich, sultry voice, then turned to Greer, "Granddaughter of Hecate," She turned to Death, "Soul collector," She smiled as her eyes landed on Brianna. "And your title will remain, Goddess, as the Guardian likes to call you. Besides, it would take too long to list your ancestors."

"It's nice to meet you, Oracle," she said, not knowing what to do. Did she bow? Curtsey? Just stand there?

"Four questions," the Oracle snapped, glancing at each of them. "One for each of you."

"Oh no." Gabe shook his head, waving his hands in front of him. "I've received enough prophecy."

"Yet, you are here, and you must ask," The Oracle said, raising her brow. "Those are the rules, and I pick the order." Her eyes landed on Death. "You first Soul Collector."

The muscle in his cheek ticked at her title for him as he crossed his arms over his chest. "Where is Boyd's soul?"

As he spoke, his words formed in a gust of smoke twisting around him before moving toward the Oracle. It made Brianna wonder what the question was that Gabe asked to lead the Oracle to announce his guardianship over her. The mist traveled up her nostrils and into her mouth. She closed her eyes as she swayed on her feet. Finally, her eyes burst open, completely white now.

"Where fire and ice have lived in darkness," she began in a gritty, rough voice. "The soul of the boy and others are held within her fists.

The descendent of darkness will be mutinous to recover them, and Death will be called to take her darkened soul to Hades for judgment."

The mist moved from her, hitting Death in the chest, making him stagger back and cough. Gabe frowned, his eyes darkening, but when Brianna glanced at him, he gave her a smile of encouragement.

The Oracle's head turned, her sky-blue eyes skimming over each of them before landing on Greer. "Now you, Granddaughter of Hecate."

Greer licked her lips. "Will I help keep Brianna and Gabe safe?" Her words twisted into smoke and again the Oracle took them in, her white eyes widening.

"You will bring Death to his knees when a decision is made," she whispered. "A choice of one, and magic will be found in words."

Greer frowned as she glanced at Death, shaking her head as the mist hit her in the chest. "I don't want to hurt you."

"She didn't say you would," he said and gave her a small smile. "Remember, she speaks in riddles and what she says usually doesn't mean what you think at first."

Greer nodded as the Oracle's eyes landed on Gabe. "Your turn, and don't ask something I've already told you. I am wise to your tricks, Guardian."

Gabe shrugged and turned to Brianna. "Before you ask, Goddess, I asked the first time I met her what I was meant to do in life and the second time I asked for more information on what I was meant to do in life. The Oracle wasn't amused."

Brianna shook her head and rubbed her forehead. "You better not push her temper. Ask a different question."

Gabe turned to the Oracle, narrowing his eyes before sighing. "Will others die by Kuraim's hands?"

The mist traveled into the Oracle.

"Returning and retreating, the souls must be saved. Many will fall, many will fail, many will live, many will die. For some, death will be a permanence. For others, it will not, but it is not all Death's choice who goes and who stays."

Gabe frowned and staggered back as the mist hit him, his brow wrinkling in confusion.

The Oracle turned to Brianna, tilting her head. "And you, Goddess?"

"Will Gabe and I live through this?" She asked. Her soul felt like it was on fire, pulling the words from her as if they were a piece of her that should have stayed forever, sliding through the Oracle's lips.

"One will live...One will fall...One will stand...One will cry. Declarations and screams...Both unheard until the breath is taken."

Brianna's soul twisted as the mist hit her, giving that piece of herself back.

The Oracle sank into a chair. "Go now," she said, abruptly waving them away with one delicate hand. "I'm tired. Don't return until the war is over, but even then, I may not be able to answer your questions."

Death nodded as black mist twisted around them again. When Brianna opened her eyes, she found herself back in her dorm room.

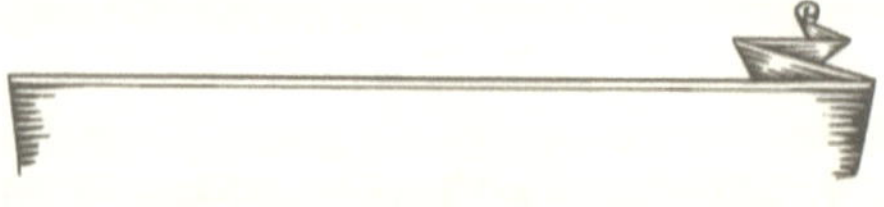

Chapter Fourteen

"I didn't understand any of that," Brianna said, pursing her lips in annoyance because Gabe had been right. Worse, she could bet on the fact he would rub this in her face. She paced across the middle of her dorm room, her arms crossed over her chest, with him tracking her movements.

"You will," Greer said, frowning as she puzzled over the prophecies. "They always come to light."

Brianna threw up her hands in frustration, stopping next to Gabe. "Well, it was all gibberish to me."

"To be fair..." Gabe smirked as he stepped closer to Brianna, "I did warn you."

Brianna shot him a quelling look as Death took out a pocket watch.

"I apologize," he said, staring at the watch, his jaw tightening, "But I don't have much time, and you owe me a chat, Brianna. I was nice to your friends. A deal is a deal."

She clenched her jaw, but she understood she couldn't go back on their deal. He had been nice, and she did owe him, no matter how much she wished otherwise.

"You can use my room," Gabe said, his lips twitching as she groaned. She narrowed her eyes at him. He grinned, knowing damn well his sudden helpful attitude annoyed her. She had a sneaking suspicion that this was revenge for going to the Oracle when he didn't want her to go. He raised his brows as he repeated Death's words. "After all, a deal is a deal, Goddess."

She curled her lip and stomped toward the door. Gabe chuckled, pissing her off even more. "Good luck, Death," he said, amusement dripping from his voice as she entered Gabe's room. "You're going to need it."

Death gave Gabe the finger before walking through the door and shutting it behind him. Brianna crossed her arms over her chest. He frowned, inhaling deeply.

"Why is your scent so strong in here?" He asked, narrowing his eyes at the rumpled sheets on the bed.

Her face screwed up in disgust. "Uh-creepy. Are you sure you don't have stalker tendencies? First, you read my mind and now you have caught my scent."

"I quit reading your mind to give you some privacy, and I'm Death." he said, shrugging. "I recognize everyone's scent."

"Still creepy." Brianna gave him an innocent smile. "It's probably so strong because I'm standing right here."

"No...You were in here last night..." he pointed his finger toward the bed. "In that bed." He sighed and shook his head. "No matter...I wanted to speak with you and hopefully dissipate your harsh feelings toward me."

She huffed. "Good luck. My mother cheated on my father with you."

A muscle twitched beneath his eye. "Should I remind you that you nor your sister would not be here without me...being with your mother?"

"That doesn't take away the fact." She pointed her finger at him. "If he found out what you were doing, it would have broken his heart."

Death raised his brow. She saw the disbelief in his eyes. She couldn't blame him. She didn't even believe her words. Larry Powers had never loved her mother, and she was equally sure her mother had never loved him.

"You know that's not true." He sighed, shaking his head. "He's always had more interest in his secretary, Susan, than your mother. He's been cheating with her his whole marriage."

Her mouth dropped open, but it wasn't in shock. He was simply confirming what she already suspected. Susan had always been near, accompanying him at work and on his trips.

He sighed as he pinched the bridge of his nose before gazing at her with eyes the same shade as her own. "It's best if I tell you what happened." He took a deep breath and blew it out. "When we were young, your mother and I wanted to marry, but Ares hated me because I was Hades' son. Hera sided with him, preventing our marriage. She's always hated Aphrodite for not falling in love with her son, Hephaestus. The punishment of her daughter delighted her. She forced her to marry the one human who wouldn't fall in love with her."

Brianna shifted, suddenly uncomfortable. It explained the odd distance she had always sensed between her parents. She couldn't even remember them embracing without other people near. "But if he found out that Sadie and I weren't his..."

Death winced. "He knows, Brianna. He has always known."

She swallowed as pain slid through her.

"I'm sorry. I understand that's harsh, but you need the truth, no matter how hard it is to hear. He had a vasectomy when he was twenty. He has never been intimate with Juliette. The only reason he signed the birth certificates was to get your mother's money, and the only reason Sadie is there and he's nice to her is his monthly allowance from your mother will stop if he's not. Sadie's powers will eventually bring her here, just like yours, but we kept you both away so Hera wouldn't punish you, too."

Brianna bit her bottom lip, trying to stop it from trembling. Somehow, she had always known that her father didn't care for her or Sadie. Maybe it was in the way he was never really there and only showed up during vacations that seemed more like photo ops. But it still hurt to have someone else confirm it.

"But *you* weren't there, either" she choked out, her soul stinging because if they knew that the man she called daddy didn't care for her, shouldn't her real father be there for her? Her eyes narrowed. "You didn't want to be around me either."

Death sighed and took a step toward her, eyes filling with tears. "You didn't see me, but I was there for everything, Brianna." She blinked, taking in the emotion on his face, trying to decide if it was real. Nothing in her life seemed to be right now. Still, her heart clenched, finding only the truth as he spoke. "I was in the audience for every school play. If you look close enough, I am in every picture during every vacation. I was even there when you took your first steps."

She frowned, her chest heavy. "But I didn't see you."

"It doesn't take away the fact that I was there, aching to be part of your life. But I wasn't allowed."

A ding sounded through the room.

He glanced down at the watch before raising his eyes to hers. "I have to go, but believe me when I say I *do* want to be near you and now that I can. I'm going to help you..." He smiled, wiping his eyes, "even if you don't want it."

She sighed, pressing the heels of her hands into her eyes, then gazed at him. "Okay," she said, her shoulders falling forward. "I'm still not calling you daddy, though. You have to earn that title."

"Any ideas on a path toward that?" He asked, letting out a relieved breath.

She nodded, her mind filling with the image of the dragon-shifter in the next room. "From what you said, Gabe is treated much like you were. Paying for the sins of his father. They think he's bad because of him. Be nice to him. It will be a step toward a relationship with me."

He chuckled. "That won't be hard. I've always liked him."

"But when I got hurt—"

"My daughter was hurt while under his care." He shrugged. "Anyone who cares for their child would be upset at whoever was in charge, whether they liked them or not."

She nodded, understanding as her eyes strayed toward the door. "He feels alone. Like the black sheep of the mythos."

"I know the feeling." He mumbled, his gaze dark with memories she wanted to know more about. "I'll try to remember that when I speak to him."

She nodded as the black mist began to engulf him, slithering up his body. "Call out my name if you need my help."

"I will, Death."

He disappeared, taking most of her anger with him.

GABE AND BRIANNA STOOD in the middle of the gym. Sweat drenched both of their bodies as he circled her on the mat. After three hours of training, three hours where she had learned little, his frustration was starting to show.

"Go for my eyes, my groin," He held his arms out. "Go for something vital. *Anything.*"

She chewed her bottom lip as the image of her breaking one of the frat boys' arms at the elbow entered her mind. "Can't we go back to the swords?" At least with them she only had to jab near his body, not actually attack it. She didn't want to hurt him.

"No, we can't," he groaned, wiping a hand over his eyes. "If someone attacks you without a weapon, you need to know what to do. We can't leave you vulnerable because you could die. You do understand that, right?"

"I-I don't want to..."

He peeled off his shirt, wiping his face with it, cutting off any other thought forming in her brain. She took in his chiseled chest and defined abs.

At her pause, he glanced at her with a raised brow. "You've got to quit getting distracted." He frowned, but she swore there was a hint of pride in his eyes. "If you don't, you will die."

He tossed his shirt away as she blinked, moving her eyes to his face. "I'm not distracted," she mumbled, knowing those words were a lie.

His lips lifted in a crooked grin. "Really?" He rubbed his hand down his eight-pack, wiping away some of the icy sweat. His skin glistened. Her eyes immediately caught on to the action, and she had to tear them away from him.

As soon as she glanced at the wall where the weapons hung, she heard him move toward her so fast that she didn't realize what he was doing. She landed on her back, her breath knocked from her. She gasped, realizing she was pinned beneath his sweaty body on the mat. Her body trembled, but it wasn't from his ice-cold sweat.

She glared at him, trying to hide her reaction to him.

His lips twitched into a cocky grin. "See? Distracted."

"Get off me." She pushed into his chest, relishing the slick muscles beneath her fingertips. "You're sweaty."

He reached up and rubbed his hand through his hair, dripping ice on her before laughing and rising to his feet.

"Come on," he said, bouncing from one foot to the other as she stood. "If you try to hit me one time, we can stop for the night. I'll even let you come watch another movie with me. Your choice...Just don't drool on my shoulder when you fall asleep this time."

She curled her hands into fists and rushed, raising her knee. Gabe easily blocked her with his leg. He smiled, grabbing her wrists, spinning her around and crossing them over her chest. He pulled her against him, trapping her in his arms, her back to his front.

"Good try," he said in her ear, his breath caressing her skin, causing her to fight back a shiver. "Tomorrow, I want to see you get out of this hold, even if you have to use your gifts."

"I don't want to hurt you," she admitted, softly.

"You won't, Goddess." He loosened his hold and turned her to face him. "Is that why you don't want to spar with me?"

"I know it doesn't seem like I could..." she nibbled on her bottom lip, "but I really did severely hurt those boys at the frat party."

His eyes widened, and he nodded. "I heard about that, but trust me. You won't hurt me. You must learn to defend yourself without Ares telling you what to do. If you don't, I'll have to worry about you the whole time I'm fighting some monster."

She sighed. "Okay."

"Go take a shower and change." She nodded and walked toward the locker room.

"And Goddess?" He called. She glanced over her shoulder, using the opportunity to take in his sculpted body one more time. "As an incentive, if you make me sweat, I will take off my shirt so you can check me out easier."

"I wasn't—"

"Don't lie, Goddess." He grinned as she blushed. "I've caught you ogling me twice in the last half hour. I should feel objectified." He put his hand on his chest as if offended. "It's okay though. I checked out your ass twice. We're even."

Her mouth dropped open, but there was nothing she could say to defend herself.

"Go take a shower," he laughed. "I'll be in the boy's locker room doing the same. I'll meet you back out here. Don't leave without me."

She nodded and turned, embarrassed, rushing into the girl's locker room to shower and change.

"YOU DID WELL TODAY, Goddess," Gabe said as they stepped through the gym doors and into the courtyard. "You faced your fear, and that's a big part of protecting yourself."

"I still need practice."

"I think you just want to see me with my shirt off."

She jerked her head up to find him grinning down at her.

A blush crept up her face, but a sudden gust of wind blew, making her shiver.

"It's not even been twenty-four hours and you've already replaced me?" the ominous voice echoed. Neva stepped from the shadows. Her ice-blue eyes slid from Gabe to land on Brianna.

Gabe stiffened and pushed Brianna behind him, blocking her from Neva. He glanced down at a ratted *Billy Idol* t-shirt beneath his trench. "Bloody hell! This is my favorite shirt." His eyes narrowed as Neva's body twitched before shifting into a great, blue-scaled beast. Her immense wings flapped, creating enough wind to almost knock Brianna over.

"Run to the dorm," he said through clenched teeth as he shook off his trench. It landed at his feet. "Stay away from our tails and, well...obviously, our ice."

She nodded as Gabe stepped away from her and shifted. His dragon exploded from him, darker than a summer sky and all sharp lines. A fierce roar beckoned her to move.

She straightened, running past them only to be stopped by a low-flying dragon. She fell on her back. Fire shot toward her. She dodged behind a marble statue of Medusa. A tremble moved through her as she peeked around the statue just as a stream of fire slammed into Gabe's chest.

Panic seized her as she screamed out the only name she knew would come. "Death!"

Black mist and smoke billowed over the ground and encompassed the two attacking dragons. A moment later, they disappeared. She glanced at Gabe, back in his human form, and lying naked on the ground. She rushed to him. He shuddered violently. Death had yet to show up. She gripped his trench to drape it over him, then gasped. A burning hole sizzled in the middle of his chest, sparking around the edges. Tears burned her eyes as she knelt beside him, the idea of his loss creating a hole in her own chest that grew bigger by the second.

"Goddess," he whispered, his voice weak. "Go."

A lump formed in her throat, tears trickled down her face. She laid the trench over him, trying to figure out a way to save him. Her knee brushed something hard on the ground. She frowned, picking up a knife. She'd seen the knife before. The memory of his blood sliding down her throat to heal her entered her mind. Would her blood do the same for him? She slid the knife over her wrist without a second thought and pressed it to his lips. Several seconds passed before his tongue snaked out to take a taste. His eyes flew open as a light burst from each of their chests.

"Brianna!" Death's voice reached her as he materialized, his eyes wide, looking at the hole in Gabe's chest. His eyes closed once more.

"There was a light..." she whispered, confused because the hole wasn't healing.

Death nodded numbly as his eyes darkened. "What type of bond would you accept to save him?"

"Any," she choked out over her sobs, clasping her hands in front of her. "Just please, save him."

He pulled a chord from his pocket and moved toward them, taking the knife from Brianna and slicing Gabe's wrist before pressing Brianna and Gabe's wounds together and binding the cord around them. "Zeus accepted, and I, as your father, do also accept," he said, his voice rough, but his eyes were filled with sadness. "For a year and a day, you are bound. May your soul heal his."

Immediately, the hole in Gabe's chest began to close. "It worked," Brianna breathed out as relief washed over her. "What did you do?"

Death winced and glanced warily at her. "I accepted the marriage contract you began when you shared your blood with him."

Gabe groaned as his eyes opened and settled on her. "Fuck, Goddess. What did you do?"

She gazed at her father, confused.

"She married you and saved your life."

Brianna's eyes widened in panic. "I'm...I'm married!"

"Hell, Goddess," Gabe said, closing his eyes once more. "I guess now you can check me out anytime you want."

Chapter Fifteen

"What the hell happened?" Greer asked, her wide-eyed gaze darting from Brianna's stunned face to Gabe dressed in only his long trench buttoned up the front. She narrowed her eyes and crossed her arms over her chest. "What did you do to her?"

"I protected her," he said, sliding his eyes to Brianna before shrugging, fighting a grin. "I guess I did well. She married me."

Brianna blinked, still stunned. "I-I didn't mean to," she said in a small voice.

Gabe put his hand over his chest at her horrified expression. "Don't be like that, love. You're going to break my heart."

"Gabe, go get dressed," Death said, his face shadowed by his cloak, but his voice was sharp. "One false move and we'll all see—"

"Heaven? Nirvana? Something to make you have low self-esteem?" Gabe finished for him, waggling his eyebrows.

Death growled. Gabe chuckled, unfazed by Death's show of anger, then turned to Brianna with a wink. "I'll be right back, wifey."

"Don't call me that!" Brianna said, her eyes wide in panic.

"But that's what you are." Gabe backed to his door with his grin sliding further up his cheeks, blowing her a kiss.

"For a year and a day," Death growled. "If you're alive that long."

"Awww...Why be that way?" Gabe laughed. "I adore all of you."

He reached back and turned the knob, walking into his room and closing the door behind him.

Greer turned to Brianna, placing her hands on her hips. "Brianna, what did you do?"

She shook her head, still looking confused. "We were attacked by dragons. They hurt him, burning a hole in his chest. I called for Death. When he didn't come, I thought if Gabe's blood healed me..."

"Oh, no." Greer paled as her eyes moved to Death. "But a union like that would have to be approved by the gods and a...a parent."

"Zeus approved it," Death said, shifting, his cheeks reddening. He tried to hide his face in the shadows of his hood, to no avail. "And it was either I accept it or my daughter's guardian would die, which would put her in danger. So, for a year and a day, they will be married."

Greer groaned and put her face in her hands. "She really needs to be taught the rules. She has barely gone to class. We've got to catch her up before she does something else."

Gabe entered the room, still smiling. "I agree. There's no harm in this though."

"I'm married." Brianna grimaced. "I'm sixteen. I won't be seventeen until April sixth and that's still too young to be married."

"There have been some gods and goddesses who were married younger," Gabe said, shrugging. "Besides, now, you can say your first husband was extremely sexy."

"You're going to enjoy this, aren't you?" Greer asked, narrowing her eyes at him.

Gabe laughed. "Every single minute."

Greer shook her head. "I'm calling Skyler," she groaned as she faced Brianna, placing a hand on her shoulder. "We're giving you a crash course on the rules, so you don't make any more mistakes."

"I am *not* a mistake," Gabe argued, as if offended, then turned to Brianna with a twinkle in his eyes. "I think she's jealous."

Death pulled his hood from his head, rolling his eyes. "Call Skyler before he gets worse."

"This is your fault too," Brianna said, facing her father.

"Did you want him to die?" Death asked, raising a brow.

"Not then," she said, her breath hissing through her teeth, "Maybe now."

Gabe simply laughed. "It's only the first day. You've got a year left."

Death narrowed his gaze. "Not if she kills you first." He shrugged one cloaked shoulder. "And I will be more than happy to hide the body."

Greer's phone dinged. She glanced down at it. "Skyler's on his way," she said, her shoulders falling forward. "I hope you're in for a long night."

Brianna threw up her hands. She couldn't imagine things getting much worse. "What else can I accidentally do?"

Gabe's smile faded as his eyes narrowed, taking on a faraway expression. "Let's just say there are worse things than marriage to yours truly. You could accidentally destroy the world.

She inhaled sharply at his serious tone and her hands began to shake. Her new life was becoming more complicated than she could have ever imagined.

SKYLER WALKED INTO the dorm room, his face pinched into a frown as his eyes moved over Gabe and Brianna.

"What happened exactly?" He asked, running his hand through his dark hair before raising his head to stare at them with irritation twisting the features of his face.

"I saved her life, and she forced me into marriage," Gabe said, laughing when she elbowed him in the ribs, causing him to take a step away from her. "I understand I'm sexy, but it's rude. She could have at least taken me to dinner first."

Skyler's lip curled. "You do realize we're still grieving, our friend," Skyler snapped, his eyes flashing. "His soul is still missing. We don't need this right now. I realize you didn't know Boyd, but he was our friend. He was important to us."

"It's not like I did it on purpose," Brianna defended herself, wincing at the pain. Whether she knew Boyd well or not, she still counted him as a friend. His absence still hurt her.

Gabe straightened, his teeth clenched. "Sit down, mutt." He rolled his eyes when Skyler growled. "Oh, get off it. I promise my growl is much louder and my bite is much scarier than yours, dog. Don't treat her like that again."

Brianna's heart squeezed. After all the teasing, he was still defending her. She frowned, her mind caught on one word. "Why did you call him a mutt?"

"Well, pumpkin," Gabe said, touching the tip of her nose with his fingertip, grinning when she swatted his hand away, "Skyler here is a god's grandson...That particular god being Fenrir, son of Loki and werewolf. Skyler can go wolfy on us at any time."

Skyler rolled his eyes as Brianna tried to imagine his boyish good looks covered with fur, but she couldn't bring up the image.

"Stuff it," Skyler growled.

"Oooo...Scary," Gabe said, faking a shiver. "Okay, before wolf boy gets riled up and starts humping legs and shedding fur, let's teach my sweet bride what she should or should not do. After all, the next time may not be so pleasurable."

Skyler growled again, but Greer hit his shoulder, pointing at a chair. "Sit!" she ordered, shaking her head. "And try to remember Brianna is new to this world. She didn't mean to do this."

"That's right. Sit like the good pup you are," Gabe said, grinning when Skyler sat down, still glaring at him. "Listen to the teacher."

Gabe turned to Greer as if she were the teacher in the middle of a class. Greer shook her head and opened her mythology book and began to teach Brianna the mysteries of the world she was now a part of.

Chapter Sixteen

"I can't believe she fell asleep." Skyler's growl of annoyance pierced Brianna's consciousness, but the only indication that she had heard him was a moan forced from between her lips.

Greer and Skyler had hammered the rules into her mind all night until everything blurred together into nonsense. Her eyelids became heavy as everything that had happened to her crashed down around her and it was no longer possible to keep her eyes open.

"She's fucking exhausted," Gabe snapped, his voice dangerously low. "Have you any idea what she's been through since she got here? She had no idea that she was a goddess, nor did she know the man who raised her wasn't her father. Everything she thought was true about her life was a complete lie...The truth covered by people she trusted, and now, she's suffered attacks from beings she didn't even know existed. She was thrown into this. Give her a bloody break."

Brianna tried to open her eyes as her bed shifted, but they refused to budge. A moment later, she felt weightless as she was pulled into the comforting coolness of Gabe's arms.

"What are you doing?" Greer asked, her voice edging in panic.

"I'm taking her to my room to *sleep*," Gabe answered, pulling her closer, his mint and ice scent surrounding her. "If I leave her in here, you wankers will try to wake her up to cram bloody knowledge down her throat that she's too tired to comprehend. However, I'm sure the moment she forgets something, you'll be quick to blame her."

"Gabe—" Death began in a placating tone.

"Don't try to stop me," Gabe hissed, his muscles tensing around her. "You wanted me to protect her from anything that could hurt her. That's what I'm doing. She needs sleep or she'll end up hurting herself. If that happens—"

"You're right," Death said softly, interrupting him from his rant. Gabe's body relaxed as he pulled her closer. His heart thrummed beneath her ear, comforting her further.

The sound of the door closing behind them fell around her a moment later. Then Gabe laid her on the soft mattress of his bed. A blanket covered her. The moment his arms pulled away from her made her moan in protest. He kissed her forehead, then wrapped her in his arms, curving his body around her back, as if protecting her from the beings next door. Her heart squeezed. She wanted to thank him but could only manage another moan.

He gently kissed the back of her head. "Sleep, Goddess," Gabe whispered to her as his arms tightened around her. She drifted further into the abyss as his words followed her into sleep. "I won't let anything hurt you...Not even them."

SHE AWOKE TO LIGHT streaming through the window with Gabe's arms still around her. Blinking, she stretched. His arms tightened, pulling her against him as he mumbled in his sleep.

"Sleep...Goddess," he whispered, his voice husky. She frowned, wondering how long he had stayed up comforting her before falling asleep. Her chest tightened as warmth spread through her.

Slowly, she turned in his arms, taking in his face in slumber. His expression was once again peaceful, a lock of his almost white hair falling over his brow. Her eyes roamed over every inch of his angelic face as she tried to figure out the mysteries about him. What drove him to protect her? Was it truly because he wanted to prove himself? She had assumed that, but he could keep her safe without being so nice to her.

She swallowed, reaching up, and brushed his hair from his forehead with the tips of her fingers. Immediately, his eyes opened, and she jerked back. He caught her wrist, his eyes darkening in a way that twisted her heart. There was a vulnerability there that spoke of how long he had been alone without someone to care for him. She frowned as an image of him as a little boy alone, in the darkness came to mind.

"Sorry," he said, shaking his head as his brow lowered over storm darkened eyes. "I'm not used to—"

"Someone being affectionate?" She asked, her heart weeping for him.

He pressed his lips together and nodded, swallowing before releasing her wrist. "I just didn't want you to think I was mad."

Her eyes met his conveying warmth and reached forward again, slowly, so he knew exactly what she intended to do. He swallowed as she brushed her fingertips against the stray locks, pushing them back into place. He closed his eyes as her fingers brushed his cheek and took a deep breath.

"Neva wasn't affectionate with you?" She asked, her voice hinting at the tenderness she experienced when near him.

His eyes opened, darkening at the mention of his ex's name, and she immediately wished she hadn't uttered a word about her. "Neva wasn't affectionate with anyone...Well, except Aidan."

"I'm sorry," she placed her hand on his chest. She felt his heart thumping wildly beneath her palm.

"And why are you being affectionate with me, Goddess?" He asked, his eyes searching her face for the answer. Hope and dread caused him to tense before she spoke.

"You cared about me when no one else seemed to," she whispered. "That means a lot to me."

"You heard them last night?" His eyes met hers, still searching for the meaning behind her actions.

She nodded. "They only seemed to care about what I have to learn." She bit her bottom lip. His eyes moved to the action. Her stomach clenched in the most delicious way. "I understand it's important, but I was only able to take in so much. You were the only one who noticed how exhausted I was...Or cared."

"It's not that they don't care," he said, his grip tightening on her waist. "They are afraid and grieving. Sometimes, those emotions are all-consuming and it's hard to show that you care."

She tilted her head, studying him, wondering if he had been afraid and grieving before. If he had, the realization that he did so alone hurt her soul deep. She leaned toward him, meeting his eyes, wishing she could take away his pain.

He licked his lips. "I'm going to kiss you now, Goddess," he said, causing her heart to speed up. He waited, his eyes moving over her face, only moving forward when she nodded.

His lips touched hers. She gasped, his icy breath mixed with the fire racing through her body. His tongue touched hers, wrapping around it as she pressed her chest to his, wanting him closer. He gripped her t-shirt in the back, slipping his fingers beneath to touch her skin there, sending tingles down her spine.

"Goddess," he whispered against her lips as she trembled against him.

She leaned into his body again, wanting more, but a knock at the door shattered the moment. She reluctantly moved away from him, her cheeks heating as she glanced at the door.

"It's okay," he said, his smile tilting across his face, erasing all the tenseness from before. "A kiss is hardly scandalous for married couples."

She groaned when she saw the mischievous glint in his eyes. "You aren't going to tease me today too, are you?"

"Well, yeah," he said as she stood and walked to the door. He chuckled. "Of course, you could kiss me to shut me up."

She shook her head, her face burning, and pulled open the door. Her eyes widened. "Mom?" Brianna winced as she glanced toward Gabe before turning back to her mother.

"I think we need to talk," her mother said, raising her brow, her lips pressed into a tight line.

Brianna's stomach twisted. Judging from the expression on her mother's face, she knew that the conversation was not going to be pleasant.

JULIETTE POWERS WALKED into the room. Her jasmine scent twisted through the air, emitting a power Brianna had never noticed before. Maybe it was because she now knew she was a goddess. Juliette's blue eyes narrowed, taking in the rumpled covers on the bed before casting her gaze at Brianna and Gabe, appearing relieved when she realized they were fully clothed.

"Let's address the huge elephant in the room," she said, twisting her hands in front of her, reminding Brianna that she was the same mother she had always known. "You two are married for a year and a day...or longer."

Brianna frowned, her mind snagging onto the last part of her mother's statement. "What do you mean, longer?" Her hands curled into fists. She was so tired of being in the dark about everything. Did they expect her to accept it without question? That wasn't going to happen.

Juliette rubbed her forehead with her fingertips. "Hera isn't fond of my mother." She sighed as her eyes lifted to meet Brianna's. "Therefore, she isn't fond of me or you. Zeus may have chosen to accept your marriage, but Hera chooses whether an annulment is accepted after the year and a day is over."

"Do you mean she may force us to remain married?" Brianna asked, her eyes wide as she moved toward the bed. "How is this legal? I'm only sixteen!"

"You are only a little over a month and a half from your seventeenth birthday, Brianna," she said, twisting her hands faster than before. "Many gods and goddesses marry at your age. Hera won't see a problem, so I doubt that your objection because of your age will mean anything to her. Neither will your ignorance of the rules. Honestly, the more miserable you seem together, the more Hera will want to permit your marriage to continue. So, it would be best if you were friends, and she witnessed that."

"We *are* friends," Brianna said, sighing in relief as she sank onto the bed. Gabe reached out and grasped her hand.

Juliette's gaze landed on their intertwined hands before it hardened, and she turned to Gabe. "Just because you are her husband, for the time being, doesn't mean that you get to take advantage of her virtue."

Gabe frowned, then his eyes widened as he took in Brianna's face. He jerked his head back to her mother. "Are you saying she's a bloody virgin?"

"Hey!" Brianna said, blushing, mortified her mother could speak so candidly about her sex life...Or lack thereof. "I'm right here. You're talking about me as if I'm not and saying things that are...private."

Gabe's mouth fell open as his gaze moved to her. "But you're a virgin?"

Brianna scowled as anger swept through her. It was insulting. He was surprised.

"It's not his fault he's in shock, Brianna." Her mother said. "Aphrodite and her descendants tend to...fall into lust easily. Even I—"

"Stop!" Brianna shouted, placing her hands over her ears. "I don't want to know."

Juliette coughed, then nodded. "Anyway, you've kept your virtue longer than most in Aphrodite's line."

"And I intend on keeping it for a while longer," Brianna said, her cheeks flushing even redder as she removed her hands from her ears. "So, can we get off this subject?"

Her mother nodded. "But you and Gabe will be expected to share a bed. You need to at least act like you are happy to be with one another, otherwise Hera won't—"

"I get it!" Brianna said, glancing down at her hands. "Moving on!"

"I just want to make sure you aren't careless again," Juliette said, causing Brianna to jerk, her stomach twisting with embarrassment and shame.

Gabe narrowed his eyes at her mother, his nostrils flaring as a flash of blue tinted his skin. "She wouldn't have been careless if you had listened to me," Gabe said, lip curling. "She knows *nothing* about us, and that's your fault. Everything she's done, including this marriage, is on you."

Juliette flinched, nodding. "Perhaps."

Brianna shifted, anger, hurt, and shame swirling through her. "Why didn't you tell me?" Brianna asked, her lip trembling. "You let me think I was crazy after those fraternity guys attacked. You could have told me then or in Sam's office the first day. You could have told me any time during my life, but you didn't."

"I wanted you to have a normal, mortal life until I couldn't hide it anymore," she said, twisting her hands in front of her again. "I would have had to tell you when you quit aging, but it was worth it to give you those years without having to face all of this."

"Are you going to tell Sadie?" Brianna asked, her nostrils flaring as she realized her little sister would have to go through the same thing...Or worse.

Juliette nodded. "When she turns sixteen."

"So, she can make the same mistakes I did?" Brianna asked, shaking her head. "Look at what has happened in three days. Don't do that to her. Tell her now, or I will."

"Not when the school is in danger," Juliette said, straightening. "It's bad enough you are here in the midst of it."

"Fine, but as soon as it's safe, you will tell her," Brianna said, raising her chin.

Juliette's eyes flashed. "Okay," she said through clenched teeth.

"So, is that all you came to do, Mother?" Brianna asked, annoyed as she crossed her arms over her chest. "Complain that I wasn't privy to the rules and ended up married or to tell him I'm a virgin?"

"No." Juliette sighed, her expression softening. "I wanted to talk to you yesterday, but Death asked me not to. So, I came today to ask you to give your father a chance. I realize you're angry, but he does love you."

"It's going to be awhile before we have any sort of father daughter relationship." Brianna's eyes flashed. "But right now, I like him better than you, so that's progress."

Juliette flinched. "I understand that. But I love you as much as I always have, and I do want to help. When you are ready to accept that, let me know, but don't hurt your father because you're mad at me."

The softness in her mother's eyes made Brianna's anger cool. She tilted her head, studying her.

"You still love him, don't you?"

"I can't remember a time when I didn't," she said softly, giving Brianna a sad smile.

Brianna nodded. She took a deep breath. "Don't lie to me anymore, and I'll try. That's all I'm promising."

"I won't. I'll come back in a few days when you've had time to think. Then we can talk about some things."

Brianna frowned as her eyes swept over her mother. She loved her...She always would but keeping secrets from her felt like a betrayal.

"Don't think this will be fixed quickly. You've lied to me about who I was my whole life."

Juliette sighed. "I didn't think it would." She opened the door and walked out, closing it behind her, leaving Brianna and Gabe in a room so silent it was suffocating.

Chapter Seventeen

Gabe raised his brows as Brianna shifted on the bed, covering her now crimson face with her hands. She sensed his gaze raking over her as he sat beside her. Her embarrassment and anxiety settled in the pit of her stomach as the silence stretched between them.

"So..."

His voice made her jump. "Don't," she moaned, shaking her head, the heat in her face rising even more as her words tumbled from her. "This is not something we need to talk about...*Ever.*"

"Forgive me, Goddess," he shifted closer to her as he spoke, "You're sleeping in my bed and less than half-hour ago, we were snogging. So, it is something we need to talk about."

She pressed her lips together, but she could tell from his expectant expression that he wasn't going to give up until she talked about the most embarrassing thing her mother brought up.

Brianna sighed. "I'm a virgin." Her voice was casual, but her hands shook, giving away how nervous she was. "I'm not giving that up until I'm mar—" she stopped, eyes widening.

Gabe grinned, his eyes flashing with amusement as he chuckled. "Married?" He was laughing hard enough to grab his stomach. She narrowed her eyes. He pressed his lips together, but they still twitched.

Seeing her humiliation, he took a deep breath, composing himself with his hands fisted in his lap. She realized he was as nervous about the topic as she was.

"Listen, that ship has sailed but I want you to know I don't care, and I wouldn't expect you to...But I have to ask...Please tell me that you've hit some of those bases so I don't feel I'm corrupting you."

She nodded, her cheeks stinging. "Second...half-way to third." She forced her gaze to his face.

"Nice to know," he said, smirking, then leaned forward and lowered his voice. "It shouldn't embarrass you, Goddess."

"You didn't help." She hit his shoulder with the palm of her hand. "You were in shock, and I thought—"

He frowned, his eyes darkening. "You thought what?"

"That you regretted the kiss this morning."

A smile played across his lips. "How could I regret something so perfect?" He tucked a strand of hair behind her ear and leaned close. She closed her eyes, expecting another kiss.

The phone dinged, preventing his lips from touching hers. He groaned as he stood and picked it up, frowning at the message.

"Well, Goddess," he said, rolling his eyes as he bounced on the balls of his feet nervously. "We need to get dressed. Sam wants to try to decipher the Oracle's prophecies."

She rose from the bed. "Okay," she said, walking to the door that separated his room from hers, relieved the discussion of her lack of sexual experience was over. She grasped the knob.

"Goddess?"

She turned around, his lips crashing into hers, taking her breath away. He wrapped her in his embrace, pulling her bottom lip between his teeth. A moment later, he pulled away, breathless.

"I'll see you in a few minutes," he said, reaching past her and opening the door, gently shoving her through. He flashed a smile, mischief sparkling in his eyes. "I'll miss you, pumpkin."

She shook her head, but with the coolness of his lips still fresh upon her own, she found she was unable to work up the annoyance for a retort.

GREER, GABE AND BRIANNA walked across the campus to the school to meet Sam, Skyler and Death in Sam's office. Brianna was surprised to see the students walking around as if it was a normal day. It disturbed her. Was it normal for them? Was danger a common occurrence at the school, and they had become accustomed to it?

Brianna snapped out of her thoughts when a boy nodded at her as he passed. Gabe put his hands over her eyes, blocking the boy from view. "Nope, nope, nope. We are not starting a harem, Goddess. I am all you need." He turned and growled. "Married woman!"

"Are you serious?" Brianna asked, her voice high-pitched, and her face crimson when he removed his hands. He put his arm over her shoulder before kissing her temple in front of the boy. He chuckled, and she elbowed him in the ribs. "I thought you had stopped this."

He grinned, his eyes becoming lighter in the bright sunlight. "Stop? I've just gotten started." He flashed his teeth in a mischievous grin. "Wait until our annulment. I'm thinking of having one of those divorce parties. We'll go all out, Goddess."

"That's *if* Hera lets you have an annulment, and that's a big *if*." Greer raised her brow when he glared. "With how angry she is at Aphrodite, you two may be hitched for eternity."

"Why do you have to ruin the fun, Greer?" He groaned before his eyes widened. "Do you go around stealing birthday presents too? You *do*, don't you?"

She shrugged. "Only if they're the good ones."

She pulled open the door, leading them into the school. As soon as they were in the hallway, Gabe dropped his arm from Brianna's shoulders, sliding his fingertips down her skin to grab her hand. Death and Skyler were waiting outside Sam's office door. Death's eyes caught on their intertwined hands, and he smirked.

"Hello, daddy-in-law!"

Death groaned as if in agony and rolled his eyes before they settled on Brianna. "How do you feel about being a widow? We'll find another way to protect you."

"Sorry." She gave him a smile. "You can't kill him."

Gabe's grin widened as he waggled his brows. "See? She likes me."

His hand tightened around hers. Death shook his head as he led them into Sam's office. Brianna's mouth dropped open. Papers were strewn across the desk and books were stacked on the chairs and on the floor.

"What happened here?" She breathed out, glancing around the small room.

Sam shook his head. "I've been trying to decipher what Death told me of the prophecies Grandmother gave you."

"And have you?" Brianna asked, leaning against Gabe's side.

Sam nodded, then turned to Gabe. "The first thing I did was take the first question and the clues my grandmother gave you. I did figure out something." Gabe shifted against her body, charging the air with nervous energy as his skin became colder. "Gabe, you suspect where the soul is. I know you don't want to believe it and are searching for a way for it not to be true, but everything points to Boyd's soul being there, along with others."

Gabe's body stiffened next to her. "What is he talking about?" Brianna asked, glancing up at Gabe as his face darkened with such heartbreak that her chest hurt.

He pressed his lips together as Sam continued nodding at Brianna. "Your suspicion spoken aloud may save her life, as well as Brianna's. You seem to care about her. Do you want her to die?"

Gabe licked his lips, a tremble traveling through his body. His eyes flicked toward Brianna, affection, and pain swirling in their ice-blue depths before he took a breath and turned back to Sam. "When Death asked where Boyd's soul was, the Oracle said, *Where fire and ice have lived in darkness, the soul of the boy and others are held within her fists.*

The descendent of darkness will be mutinous to recover them, and Death will be called to take her darkened soul to Hades for judgment. It brought to mind that Aidan is fire, and I am ice. We lived in Mid-Veil with our mother in darkness...A cave. The darkness was to prevent us from looking into her eyes. That partnered with the first prophecy where it says, *Twin souls of light and night face the one where evil began.* Aidan and I are far from twin souls, but he was always called light, and I was called night, so perhaps, because we are brothers, we are considered so in prophecy. Evil began in Mid-Veil. It's where the first murder took place."

"So, you suspect your mother?" Brianna asked, her heart aching from the distraught expression in his eyes. "Why didn't you tell me?"

"She's always been cruel and awful, and I understand why everyone assumes it would be easy to hurt her." His voice cracked with emotion as a tremble slid down his body. "But she's still my mum, and she and Aidan are still the only family I have. Aidan's gone...Letting go of her would leave me alone."

"That's not true, Gabe." Skyler surprised them when he took a step toward him. "I understand where you are coming from. I faced the same thing two years ago when my mother's bloodlust got out of control. She hated me. She had always hated me, and I suspected her. I didn't want to turn her in. But I knew I had to. Once I realized Sam and everybody here are my family, it was much easier to do. We're your family too, Gabe."

"But you hate me." Gabe deadpanned, raising his brow as he faced the werewolf.

"Does that matter?" Skyler asked, shrugging. "Your mother hates you too, but she has your loyalty. The difference between me and her is there is a chance I won't hate you forever and I will help you even when you piss me off."

"I guess that's true." Gabe closed his eyes, taking a deep breath. He glanced at Death. "So, I guess we're going to Mid-Veil?"

"I think we have to," Death said, frowning. "Besides me, you're the only one who can navigate it. If she sees me, she will fight, then she will die. Perhaps you can talk to her. Perhaps we can reach her before Kuraim does. That way, at least she'll live."

"We'll go tomorrow," Gabe said, glancing at Brianna before releasing her hand and walking out the door. His tall frame was tense, each muscle bulging, but it was his face that revealed how hurt he was. Darkness shadowed his features, but beneath his skin was a flash of blue, showing his dragon lurking. Then he was gone.

She took a step to go after him, but Death gently grabbed her arm. "Give the boy some time." His voice was grim. "He's having trouble controlling his dragon. He realizes you're safer without him right now."

She glanced at the door. A few minutes later, a roar broke through the air, making her jump. But it wasn't a roar of anger. It was one of a broken heart.

Chapter Eighteen

The sky had turned from a bright blue to the deep, almost black of night before Gabe returned to their room. Brianna was sitting on the bed, glancing at the door every few minutes, worry twisting through her. When he opened the door, her heart leapt into her throat as her eyes raked over him, thankful he was with her, but the worry didn't completely fade. He wore different clothes, making her wonder if he had hidden them around the school in case he shifted.

He glanced away from her, hiding the pain still evident in his eyes, and shoved his hands into the pockets of his jeans while rocking back on his feet. "I didn't mean to leave for so long."

"It's okay," she whispered, wanting to comfort him but not knowing how. She shifted when he didn't say anything else. "When do we leave for Mid-Veil?"

He jerked his head up violently to stare at her with wide eyes, as if asking silently if she had lost her mind. "*We* aren't going to Mid-Veil. I am going and you are going to stay here."

She raised her brow as the first hint of anger slid through her, replacing the worry she had been wallowing in since she had left Sam's office. "What do you mean, I'm not going?"

"Exactly what I said. You are *not* going." He glared at her as she stood from the bed and crossed her arms over her chest. "You are staying her where it's safe, and you are protected."

She barked out a laugh, but there was no humor in it. "It's not safe here, Gabe." She threw up her hands. "I've almost died here, and that's with you on the same campus."

A muscle ticked in his cheek as he stepped closer to her. His chin tilted stubbornly, but she didn't back down. "It's still safer here," he said through his teeth. "This isn't like going to meet my mother in the same way as another guy. My mother is a fucking *gorgon*, which means she can kill you with a glance. Not to mention, she will not be in a good mood. She's on the gods' and goddess' shit list, and no gorgon wants to be on that. Do you know of fucking Medusa? That wasn't made up."

Brianna's chest heaved as her eyes narrowed. He had treated her like a clingy girlfriend, and it was really pissing her off. "How dare you treat me like a stupid, naïve girl who wants to trap her man by meeting his mommy and daddy." She curled her hands into fists as her face heated. "I *know* it's dangerous. I'm not stupid, but I also know being without my guardian is a death trap. Besides, finding Boyd's soul and bringing down Kuraim has just as much to do with my life and death as yours. Honestly, the only thought I had about you was simply knowing how hard this would be on you, and I wanted to be there for you."

"I don't need you there to take care of me," he growled. For a moment, she saw his dragon flash beneath his skin. "I need you far away from it. Maybe you haven't noticed, but I can take care of myself."

She stepped closer to him, nostrils flaring. "Yep. I noticed. That's why you ended up married to me...Because you can take care of yourself. I saved you. I sacrificed for you."

As soon as the words were out of her mouth, she realized she shouldn't have said them. He jerked as if she had slapped him. Then his eyes brightened, glowing in the dim room. "Well, I'm sorry my presence is such a sacrifice, Goddess," he hissed, the venom in his voice causing her to wince. "It's not been great for me, either. Putting up with a girl with enough daddy and mommy issues, Dr. Phil wouldn't be able to fix them."

She sucked in a breath, then straightened, hurt swirling through her. At that moment, she wondered if all his tender actions had been a lie. "Fine. You won't have to put up with me and my issues anymore," she said, determined to get away from him and his painful words before the stupid tears stinging her eyes showed themselves. She raised her chin and started to walk past him.

He grabbed her wrist, spinning her to face him. "You can't just fire your guardian," he said, narrowing his gaze, his face red. "The Oracle chose me. That's not something you can just ignore, Goddess."

It stung that his guardianship over her was the only thing that mattered to him. She tried to pull her wrist from him, but he held her easily, the anger and hurt mixing into her bloodstream in a toxic cocktail.

"Watch me," she hissed, lifting her eyes to his, pouring as much acid as she could into her expression. Her nostrils flared as she continued. "And watch me ignore you and this marriage, too."

A growl rumbled through his chest as he pulled her against him, wrapping his arms around her tightly. His face was an inch from hers as a shiver ran down her spine. She had pushed the beast too far and now he was close...too close. His body was ice cold against her skin, leaving traces of frost upon its surface, but fire raced through her veins. She gritted her teeth, trying to fight all the anger...all the pain his callous treatment of her had caused, as well as the lust caused by his close proximity. Need slammed through her, proving she would never be immune to him.

"You want to get rid of me, Goddess?" He rasped out, his lips so close that his cool breath touched her like a caress as his eyes moved over her face. Her breaths were coming too quickly. She swallowed because, as much as she fought it, her attraction to him was obvious. His brow raised as the tip of his nose touched hers. "No...I don't think you do."

She opened her lips to retort, but his mouth crashed down on hers, mixing his cold with her heat. Their tongues clashed as his arms tightened around her waist, pulling her closer. Though she understood she should fight her attraction to him, her body didn't get the memo. Her chest arched into him as he backed her toward the bed before they tumbled down upon it.

His hands moved down her arm before clasping her wrists and pressing them against the pillows beside her head. His teeth scraped her bottom lip, shattering her mind and making her lose focus before realizing she couldn't move her wrists. She pulled away from him and glanced at them, finding an odd glowing blue cord around them, trapping her to the bed.

He kissed her forehead before moving off her, turning his back and walking toward the door with determined steps.

"Gabe, take these off," Brianna said as panic slithered through her. He had tricked her. He was going to face his mother alone. His pain was more torture than she could describe.

He turned toward her, his eyes swimming in tears. "Greer will take them off when I've passed into Mid-Veil."

Fear seized her. She thrashed against the cords until her wrists hurt. "Please, Gabe. Don't do this," she pleaded with tears flooding her eyes as the thought of him facing the pain of betraying his mother alone caused her to buck on the bed even harder than before trying to gain release.

His face darkened as his shoulders bowed forward. Each word he spoke was laced with so much agony it caused her heart to thrum painfully against her ribs. "You may hate me...You may want to rid me from your life, but I don't want you to be gone from mine. That is exactly why you are bound to the bed. So, hate me. I'll take that over your death."

Brianna cried out for him as he walked out of the room and though she realized it should be a cry of anger, instead it was a cry of fear at the possibility that Gabe could be gone from her life forever because she knew his mother was just as dangerous to him as everyone else.

FOUR HOURS PASSED, Brianna fighting the bonds the whole time, to no avail. Panic had moved into hurt and hurt into anger so hot Brianna's whole body glowed as if she were about to fight a horde of monsters.

Greer and Skyler stepped into the room, Skyler's lips twitching as he took in her body bound to the bed. "Well, I see someone took *50 Shades of Grey* too seriously," he said, then the bastard took out his phone and took a picture.

"Take these damn things off," Brianna growled through clenched teeth as she imagined ways to torture and kill Skyler.

Greer raised a brow. "I wouldn't piss her off, Sky. She's glowing, which means she's extremely angry. She doesn't know how to control that power yet. She could really hurt you." Greer reached her hand forward, and the binds fell from Brianna's wrist.

She scrambled off the bed. "Take me to Mid-Veil."

Greer winced, her expression darkening in regret. "I can't." When Brianna took a menacing step toward her, Greer put her hands out in supplication. "Only dragons and Death know the way, and only the high gods and angels can enter besides them. Anyone else needs a dragon to accompany them."

Brianna's eyes narrowed, and she threw her head back. "Death!"

A moment later, he appeared in a cloud of black mist. His eyes widened when he saw the glow around Brianna's skin, his eyes traveling to the ties now lying dormant on the bed.

He raised a brow as he faced his enraged daughter. "I wondered how he kept you from accompanying him," Death said, sighing, "I'm glad he did so safely."

The glow around her body brightened as she took a step forward, facing her father. "Take me to Mid-Veil."

"I can only go myself. It would break the treaty to take you. I can't do that without risking a war."

Brianna pressed her hand to her eyes and let out a scream of frustration, her body practically vibrating with anger. "Bring him back here, then."

"I can't do that right now," Death cautiously walked in front of Brianna, causing Skyler to wince. Death wrapped his hands around her shoulders as his eyes searched hers. "Calm down for me so I can explain what has happened."

She closed her eyes and took two deep, slow breaths before slowly opening them again and peering at her father. Her skin tingled, but it no longer glowed. Tears shined in her eyes, causing Death's expression to soften in sympathy.

"His mother is being arrested," he said, swallowing. "She's been blinded to prevent harm to anyone else."

"Did they find Boyd's soul?" Greer asked, her eyes wide.

"They did. They found souls of mermaids, werewolves, and banshees as well. They've been delivered to Hades. Hades has sent Boyd's soul to Hela. She'll decide where he will reside."

She nodded as Skyler pulled her into his arms, hugging her as she silently cried. Death looked back at Brianna. "Gabe is understandably upset." He took a deep breath. "I realize you're mad that he didn't take you with him, but as your father. I am grateful he didn't. She turned twelve men before Gabe blinded her."

Brianna's mouth dropped open as her stomach twisted. "G-Gabe blinded his mother?"

"It was either that or she would have been killed," he said as Brianna's face fell and her heart broke in two. "So, as angry as you are, you need to understand where he was coming from. He was worried she would hurt you, but he was also facing a task that will haunt him forever. He did what he thought was best for everyone at a great sacrifice to himself."

Brianna clutched her chest as tears fell down her cheeks. It killed her. Gabe was dealing with his grief alone when she was determined never to let him feel that way again.

"Can you go to him?" Brianna asked, pleading. "Be there for him when I can't."

Death gave her a sad smile and nodded. Warmth spread through her as she realized her father truly cared. Grateful, she stepped forward and hugged him. His body stiffened in surprise before wrapping his arms around her, kissing the top of her head.

"Thank you," she said, backing away.

She faintly saw his eyes swimming with tears before the mist surrounded him and he disappeared. Even if she wasn't there, she hoped that Gabe would find some comfort in her father's presence.

Chapter Nineteen

Gabe still hadn't come back when darkness fell. Most students left, returning home until Monday. Though Kuraim and his followers were still a threat, the retrieval of Boyd's soul was enough to resume the regular school schedule, giving proof again that the students were used to the danger.

Brianna pushed her breath from between her lips and stared out the window of the room she now shared with Gabe, worry for him gnawing at her gut. Her mind offered her the image of his shoulders slumped in defeat, his soul darkened eyes filled with so much pain it caused her heart to ache. Worse, her imaginings offered people walking around him, oblivious to the despair he was in. The vast loneliness that always surrounded him was suffocating. She was going insane because of her inability to take away his pain and make it any better.

Finally, she laid down on the bed, her eyes closing as the spicy, cool cologne he wore scenting the pillows and blankets wrapped around her. Exhausted, her eyes grew heavy, and she drifted to sleep, her dreams a kaleidoscope, hinting at real people, places and events.

The bed dipping brought her back to consciousness as a cool fingertip traced down her arm. A soft kiss was placed on her forehead. Slowly, she opened her eyes in preparation for seeing Gabe's beautiful face broken by the knowledge of having to blind his own mother, but she wasn't prepared...Not at all.

Scratches marred his beautiful skin, slicing across his chest in deep, bloody grooves. But those didn't compare to the pain in his eyes. Her heart broke as she reached forward and cupped his cheek, hoping her touch capable of taking away some of his agony. His eyes closed on contact, giving her a reprieve from his heartache.

"Goddess," he whispered, brokenly, as if trying to keep a sob at bay. "I expected you to be gone."

Her heart clenched at the fact that he thought he would be alone in his misery once again. "I was mad," she whispered, wishing for the ability to take away everything she had said in that moment of desperation, "And hurt that you didn't want me to be there for you."

"I didn't want you harmed," Gabe murmured, a frown marring his brow as he struggled to speak when his emotions were swirling through him at a dangerous speed. "My mother is dangerous...even for me. She wouldn't hesitate to kill you. I couldn't bear—"

She placed a finger over his lips. "I understand. Because I couldn't bear the thought of you hurting alone."

Gabe blinked as confusion spread over his face. Her heart and soul pulsed with his pain. The realization that no one had cared about him squeezed her heart. She moved closer to him, wanting to give him comfort, but she also wanted to protect him from all the misery in his soul.

He bent down and brushed his lips across hers before wrapping his arms around her, his face buried into her hair, and in the darkness, she absorbed the touch of ice as a single tear hit her shoulder. At that moment, she realized she would do anything to take away the pain that had travelled with him his whole life. She would never allow him to experience the crushing weight of loneliness or the loneliness that came from not being cared for by anyone again. At that moment, she realized she was in love with him.

SHE HELD GABE IN SILENCE, his head resting on her chest until they both fell into an exhausted sleep.

Light caused her to open her eyes, blinking against the brightness. She found herself in a cave, the sun shining in, lighting the darkness within.

The man she had seen walking along the gate when she first arrived at the school...the same man who had stood outside the door where Boyd had died stood in front of her. She recognized him even though he had his back to her, his hands clasped behind him as if waiting patiently for something or someone.

"Kuraim," a familiar voice said, moving close to the man who Brianna now knew wasn't a man at all. This was the being Aidan, Alona and Neva followed, betraying the school and the gods as well as everyone in the world, human and mythos alike.

"Aidan," Kuraim purred, turning, his dark eyes raking over him as if searching for any reaction to his next words. "They have taken your mother. She gave them the souls. Gabriel blinded her. She's useless to us now."

"How did they find out she was helping us?" Aidan asked, a muscle jumping in his cheek, a flash of anguish quickly passing over his face, then it was gone. She wondered if he was hiding his grief at the news of his mother's capture, but then his eyes flashed as his gaze found Kuraim's. He growled before Kuraim could speak. "The damn Oracle." His eyes glowed a deep crimson. "She'll keep spewing out those prophecies, ruining everything, probably getting us killed."

"You would think that, wouldn't you?" Kuraim asked, grinning as he bent, picking up a green bag at his feet.

Brianna's eyes widened and her stomach roiled when he reached in and pulled a severed head by its long, dark hair and tossed it at Aidan's feet, causing him to jump back as the head rolled stopping with the face of it staring with glazed eyes up at him.

The Oracle's parting words to them echoed through her mind. "Don't return until the war is over but even then, I may not be able to answer your questions."

Brianna stepped forward as her breath shuddered from her, staring at the face of the Oracle now silent in her death.

The dream shattered as Kuraim laughed. "She won't be making prophecies anymore," he said as the vision ended and Brianna sat up with a sob, causing Gabe to stir and look at her with tired eyes.

"Goddess?" Gabe asked, his voice husky from sleep. A frown marred his brow when he saw her panic filled face.

She turned to him, a shiver sliding down her spine. "We have to get to the Oracle. I dreamed Kuraim killed her."

Gabe wrapped her in his arms, running his hand down her back while calling out for her father.

DEATH DIDN'T ARRIVE, and a search for Sam came up empty. Gabe had summoned Greer and Skyler after the dream and they tried to help, but they ended up sitting in Gabe and Brianna's dorm room, each trying to summon Death to no avail. Gabe was pacing, his dragon flashing beneath his skin as he cursed beneath his breath.

Three hours later, black mist moved through the room, Death appearing within it. He glanced around, his eyes dark as he took in each of their faces before landing on Brianna's. He stepped toward her, his usual stoic expression creased with worry.

"Did you dream?" He asked, his voice brittle.

She rose from the bed, eating up the rest of the distance between them. Her body shook. "About the Oracle," she whispered. "I saw Kuraim. I've seen him before...Twice since I've been here. Once at the wall when I arrived and once standing in front of the room where Boyd died. I didn't realize it was him and now, this dream...The Oracle died."

He blew out a breath. "That's why it took so long. I dreamed of her death, too, hoping I could stop it."

Her eyes roamed over his face. Tears glistened in his blue eyes. Her heart clenched. The Oracle had been his friend, and just because he was Death didn't mean he didn't experience the grief for those he loved when they passed.

Brianna swallowed, hoping his tears were for another reason. "It didn't come true, right? She's not—"

Death nodded as he swallowed, fighting back a sob. "I was too late," he choked out. "Her soul was taken. Whatever they are doing with the souls, they have a powerful one now. I can only hope she fights against whatever they are going to use her for."

His body shivered beneath his cloak, and Brianna's hands curled into fists. What good was this gift she and her father had if they couldn't save anyone? It only left them with immense guilt and sorrow.

He took a deep breath. "We need to find Kuraim and end this," he said, his teeth clenching.

She nodded, meeting his eyes. "We'll figure it out together. We may have seen the same scene, but different things. There must be a clue within our dreams."

He pressed his lips together, his shoulders bowed forward. "If you don't mind working with me..."

She frowned as she peered at him. She realized the similarities between Gabe and her father. Both were alone in their grief. The knowledge burned through her as she realized some of her father's misery was her fault. All the pain of finding out that he was her father and her life had been a lie faded away. Death had done nothing but help her and try to protect her since they met...Probably even before. She sighed. She didn't want to be mad at him anymore. She wanted to get to know him. Maybe in all the grief, simply accepting and loving each other would help.

She wrapped her arms around him and pressed her head against his chest. "Of course, I don't. You're my dad."

He stood completely still for a moment before his chest rose in a deep breath of relief and he wrapped his arms around her. When she pulled back, he kissed the top of her head. She felt a teardrop land on her skin, but this one was one born from a father's love returned by his child.

Chapter Twenty

Much to Gabe's dismay, classes had resumed. Gabe had fully healed from his mother's attack and Death and Brianna had compared their dreams. Neither found any clues that gave away the location of Kuraim.

Gabe paced their room, a frown marring his angelic face as he glanced outside, the voices of the students walking across campus drifting towards them.

"I don't think the school should be reopened yet." He scowled, glancing out the window in disgust. "It's too bloody dangerous. You'll be out there in the open. We don't know who else is working for Kuraim, which means you'll be in danger."

"You do realize there are other students in danger, right? It's not just me." Brianna raised her brow as she ran a brush through her golden blonde hair. She shrugged one shoulder. "Besides, you'll be with me. They changed your class schedule to match mine."

"You're the only one I care about, Goddess. I couldn't care less about the other students." His eyes were stormy, but his words caused her heart to flutter. "The schedule change does not make me feel better. You will be out there with *them*."

She chuckled. "So, what do you want to do, lock me in here?" The glare he shot her caused the smile to fall from her face.

"Good idea. Tell them you're sick."

She rolled her eyes and shook her head, determined not to hide out in their room. "I'm going to class. I'm already behind as it is."

His chest rumbled as his dragon flashed beneath his skin. "Fine," he said through his teeth. "But I can't promise that I won't be an overbearing asshole for the rest of the day."

"How is that different from any other day?" She quipped, chuckling when he straightened and narrowed his eyes at her.

He grabbed her bag, slinging it over his shoulder, then gripped her hand, intertwining his fingers with her own. He ground his teeth, showing his annoyance, glaring at any boy who passed them. She gave him a sidelong glance.

"You aren't going to cover my eyes again, are you?" She asked. It sounded like a joke, but she was serious.

He leaned close to her ear, a shiver trailing down her spine. "No. I'm pretty sure you know who you're with. So will everyone else," He smirked, erasing most of the darkness in his expression.

He reached into the pocket of his jeans, pulling out a student I.D. and handing it to her. She glanced down at the little plastic card, her eyes widening when she saw her picture. But the name on it was different...Brianna Isolde.

"You do know we're only married for a year and a day, right? Less than a year now?" She shook her head.

"Mmm-hmmm." He shrugged before brushing his lips against hers. "For the moment, though, you have my last name. I can honestly say I didn't do this. The school did."

"Are you going to make jokes about our marriage again today?" She asked as they made their way down the stairs.

He grinned. "Since you're forcing me to go to school and attend classes, it's my right."

Brianna groaned, waving at the security guards before stepping outside. "Fine." She didn't mind his teasing as long as he wasn't brooding.

Her smiled died on her lips when she realized the students who had been walking and joking stopped to stare at their clasped hands.

Rowen walked toward them, an amiable smile covering the viciousness in her eyes. Brianna frowned as she tried to see the banshee in Rowan's pretty face, but it was hiding too well.

Gabe stepped between them, crossing his arms.

"Not happening, hag."

"I'm supposed to apologize." Her lips twitching at his protectiveness.

"You can do it from there."

Rowan smiled, shifting slightly to see Brianna standing behind him. "I'm sorry I frightened you." Her voice was sugary sweet, but her shrug showed indifference. "But it looks like you've moved on from it." She glanced at Gabe. "I really can't hold that against you, though. Goddesses of love tend to be a bit...promiscuous. Obviously, they don't have much taste or class in who they choose to be with. Even so, I would have chosen someone much better to bind myself to in marriage."

Brianna stepped around Gabe, the rumble in his chest getting louder as his teeth sharpened, but Brianna's own temper was rising as she clenched her fists at her side. He reached for her arm, but she shrugged him away. "Rowen, I may be a goddess of love..." Her voice lowered dangerously, "but it will do you well to remember that I'm also a goddess of war, the underworld, and death."

Brianna's body flickered, and Rowen backed away, her expression showing the first hint of fear.

"Fuck, Goddess." Gabe pinched the bridge of his nose as his growls calmed, only to be replaced by a groan. "We really should have taught you the rest of those rules."

Rowan and the other students quickly moved away from them. Some were casting interested looks at her, others appeared more fearful.

"What do you mean?" She asked, her body seeming to surge with energy.

"Well, you just accepted most of your titles." He frowned. "And all the powers that go with them."

"Is that a bad thing?"

He pulled her close to his side as he started walking again. "Well, all I'll say is expect your gifts to get a lot more complicated."

"YOU DID WHAT?" SKYLER ground out as they sat at their table in the school cafeteria. For a moment, it seemed as if his eyes had turned yellow as he turned to Gabe. "Why didn't you stop her?"

"I didn't know she was going to accept her gifts and once the words were spoken, what did you expect me to do, wolfy?" Gabe said, narrowing his eyes.

Greer stared at her with an expression that mirrored Skyler's. When she spoke, her voice was solemn. "Brianna..."

"Don't tell me there isn't a way out of this," she said, glancing between the three of them. Tears burned her eyes, but she refused to shed them. She had already shed enough.

"Well, Goddess, there is..." Gabe shook his head. His face was pale as he ground his teeth. "It would take a sacrifice from your mate."

"My mate?" She frowned. "Do you mean you?"

"Not necessarily." Skyler winced. "Have you two..."

Brianna frowned. "What?" Then her eyes widened as her cheeks flamed. "No!"

"I'm sorry!" Skyler's voice rose as he put out his hands. "But it's literally the only way to transfer your gifts."

"That's not happening," Brianna's body shook. "I'm not ready for...*that*!"

"The problem is, Goddess..." Gabriel blew out a breath. "Every male and female in this school who wants to become a god or goddess will try to mate with you. Worse, some of Kuraim's followers may consider it as a way for him to become a god. Some of them may be desperate enough to try to force you."

Her eyes widened as the tears she was trying to keep at bay rose to the surface. "You mean rape?"

"Yes, but the good thing, if you can call it that, is you can only give your gifts to one mate. So, it may be best if we pretend we have." He gave her a pained smile. "I mean, we do sleep in the same bed, we share a room and we're married. Not to mention," He smirked. "I'm sexy as hell, so it wouldn't be unbelievable."

"But won't they know you aren't a god?" Brianna asked, her eyes wide.

"I think I can help with that," Greer said, chewing her bottom lip. "I can summon Hecate. She can give him a gift to protect you that would mimic a god's power. The gods and goddesses will support that because they don't want Kuraim or any other dark one to have a way into the heavens."

"Why do you seem worried?" Brianna narrowed her eyes as she studied her.

"Because...well...everyone here must be respectful." She blew out a breath. "My grandmother isn't a goddess you want to be rude to."

Everyone turned to Gabe.

His mouth dropped open, offended, as he placed his hand on his chest. "I can be downright gentlemanly if need be."

Greer laughed. "Well, dragon boy, you'd better." She smiled sweetly. "Because my grandmother can come up with ways of torture that would make your mother appear tame."

A muscle ticked in his cheek. "I can do it." He straightened, but worry still clouded his eyes. Then he turned to Brianna. "You owe me for this one, Goddess."

"In the meantime, read this." Greer ignored him, sliding the Mythology book toward her. Brianna rubbed her hand across her eyes, sighing as she opened the book.

Chapter Twenty-One

Brianna slammed shut the Mythological Studies book as the math teacher, Mrs. Colton, shouted her name. She ground her teeth as the woman walked up and stood in front of her, glaring with undisguised anger and hatred across her wrinkled face while the rest of the class gave her pitying glances. Brianna had been ignoring the math equations on the board to learn the rules which she had discovered could cause havoc in her life if she remained ignorant. To Brianna, learning those rules was more important than any math problem would be. Obviously, Mrs. Colton didn't feel the same.

Her lips were pressed into a thin line as she stared down her long, beak-like nose at Brianna with disgust. She didn't understand why, but from the moment the teacher had met her, she did little to hide her hatred, snapping at her for no reason or glaring whenever her beady eyes landed on her. For a moment, she wondered what creature she was. Maybe an evil little troll.

"This is not your Mythological Studies class," she hissed in a voice that reminded Brianna of nails scratching on a chalkboard as she pointed at the book on the desk with a razor-sharp fingernail. "This is Algebra."

Brianna stared at the woman, her mouth opening to defend herself, but Gabe spoke first.

"Back off, Harpy."

The woman's narrowed gaze landed on him. Gabe stared back, silently challenging her to go against him. Brianna's lips twitched because she had no doubt Mrs. Colton would lose. She tucked a strand of graying black hair behind her oddly pointed ear. A hiss moved from between Mrs. Colton's teeth.

Gabriel blinked at her, unfazed by her show of aggression. A grin slid over his face, his eyes glinting dangerously. "Remember what happened the last time harpies tangled with a dragon."

Harpy?

As Brianna's eyes roamed over her, she could see it. The woman's birdlike features were prominent, from her beak of a nose to her talon-like nails.

Mrs. Colton's eyes narrowed. "I will speak to Mr. Leo about this."

Gabe shrugged, unaffected by her threat. "And I will tell him you are preventing Brianna from studying the rules she needs to learn to prevent any danger to herself and the school." He smiled, holding up a notebook. "I'm copying notes for her, and she will be doing the work you give her. Don't single her out because she is mated with a dragon."

Brianna frowned. Mrs. Colton's hate had everything to do with Gabe and nothing to do with her? Her spine straightened as anger slithered through her.

"So unfortunate for her," she said, curling her lip in obvious disgust. Brianna's hands tightened into fists so tightly her nails were making crescent moons in her palm. "I don't know why she would choose to be with someone like you. She's a goddess and you're a scaled freak."

Brianna's head snapped up, each insult a blow to her own soul. The hatred Gabe faced each day caused the reign on her anger to snap. "Maybe it's because I can see how good he can be. How brave. How protective he is of the ones he cares about."

Mrs. Colton's spine straightened at her words as Gabe leaned toward her, his mouth hanging open before he blinked and covered his expression of awe with a face-splitting grin, his eyes sparkling.

"Thank you, Goddess." His voice was both amused and filled with affection that cooled her anger from boiling to simmering.

Mrs. Colton's face reddened as she crossed her arms over her small chest. "That still does not erase the fact that she's behind in her classes."

"She's behind because she just started this school." Gabe narrowed his eyes at her. "I have every faith that she will catch up."

"Impossible." A sneer curled the corner of her mouth. "She isn't a goddess of wisdom."

Gabe raised his brow. "True. But she is one of the goddesses of the Underworld as well as death." He smirked as Mrs. Colton's eyes widened. "That makes her your boss. You might want to remember that before she summons her grandfather or father and lets them know exactly how you're behaving."

Mrs. Colton blanched. "I'm sure the other teachers are upset, too," she said weakly. "Not just me."

"No, they've been completely understanding of the situation," he snapped. "As a matter of fact, none of them has thrown in her face how behind she is apart from you."

He rose from his desk, beckoning Brianna to follow. She stood, trying to keep her anger from rising again as she picked up her book from the desk and shoved it in her backpack.

"Where are you going?" The woman shrieked, causing Brianna's eardrums to pulse with the sound.

Gabe turned to the woman and grasped Brianna's hand. "We've had enough of your abuse. We are going to the library so she can study."

Mrs. Colton met his gaze. "You think just because you're married, she'll choose you when the year and a day is over?" She hissed, causing him to straighten. "But she'll see you for what you are. One of the fallen's offspring. Evil. Rotten."

The anger that had been simmering just a moment before rose to boiling. Brianna's chest burned as she pulled her hand from Gabe's and walked toward the woman, imagining violent things she had never entertained.

"Don't you *dare* talk to him like that." She ground her teeth together as darkness swam in her eyes, moving through her until her body was encased in the same mist that usually surrounded her father. Mrs. Colton gasped and took a step back. "You are a vile, cruel creature, and if you say one word that is out of line to him...Just *one word*...I will serve your tongue on a platter to my grandfather. Do you understand?"

The rest of the students in the class stared at them in terror. Gabe's hand tightened on hers, his shock causing his muscles to stiffen. The woman trembled, unable to speak, as she nodded quickly.

Gabe took a deep breath and stepped in front of her, blocking Mrs. Colton's offending presence from her sight, and pushed a strand of hair behind her ear before giving her a smile. "It's okay, Goddess." His voice was so soft and gentle, her heart ached. "I think you've made your point."

Her breaths were coming quickly...too quickly. Her blood flowed like lava sliding through her veins. Gabe sighed as he leaned forward and pressed his lips to hers. Instantly, her anger changed to something that caused her heart to clench. She could feel her body calm. The black tendrils faded until they disappeared completely. He pulled away from her and caressed her cheek.

"Are you alright, Goddess" He asked, softly, his eyes meeting hers.

She nodded and swallowed. "Yes," she said, but her voice was thick and breathless.

He turned toward Mrs. Colton, his icy gaze settling on her. "Be warned. I won't stop her next time," he said, his chest puffing out proudly. "It would do you well to remember that she is just as protective of me as I am of her."

Mrs. Colton nodded as he grabbed Brianna's hand and pulled her through the door. She smiled. Gabe was right. She did want to protect him as much as he wanted to protect her. As she glanced at him, she found a smile still plastered across his face. Her heart lurched. She realized until she defended him, he had not really experienced that kind of care. Until that moment, she knew he thought everyone saw him as worthless...a freak. She took a deep breath, promising that she would always show him his worth and no one would ever hurt him again without retribution.

BRIANNA FROWNED AS she read another seemingly ridiculous rule in the book. "Why?" She mumbled to herself, causing Gabe to raise his head and peer at her with a raised brow.

"What do you mean, why?" He asked, his lips twitching in amusement.

"Why is Hera so protective of her apples?" She moaned, rubbing her temples.

Gabe's lips curled into a grin. "They were a wedding present from her mum." He shrugged. "Each tree with different supernatural gifts. She is protective of it because people and gods alike have taken advantage of those gifts."

"You sound like you know a lot about her." Brianna leaned toward him, suddenly interested in the goddess who prevented her mother and father from marrying and who now had control of how long Gabe and Brianna would remain in matrimony.

"Well, Ladon protects her apple orchard, and he's a dragon. So, dragons know about it."

Brianna smiled. "I guess all dragons guard something."

Gabe's face darkened. "Ladon is in love with Hera. He could never act on it because Zeus would punish him, but he would do anything for her...That includes guarding her precious orchard."

"Are you saying he's actually *her* guardian, not the grove's?" Brianna asked, tilting her head.

Gabe shifted, then nodded. "He's a cautionary tale about dragon guardians falling for one of the gods. It usually doesn't work out well."

Brianna frowned. Even though her marriage with Gabe would end after the year and a day, she was already attached to him. She didn't want their relationship to end. She wanted it to continue and choose their own path, but it seemed that everyone was betting that they would fail before they had even begun.

Gabe moved closer to her, sensing her distress. His lips touched her ear. "It's a good thing I don't heed caution."

She turned toward him, blushing because it seemed he had pulled her thoughts from her mind. He leaned toward her, his cool breath touching her lips, causing her heart to pick up speed.

"Any danger of a broken heart is worth it with you." His cool breath was like a caress on her skin.

His lips touched hers as Greer's voice echoed through the library, not allowing more than a peck. They both turned toward her, glaring at her in annoyance.

"Get a room." She rolled her eyes.

"I thought you were smart, Greer." Gabe clucked his tongue and swept his arm, indicating the library. "This *is* a room."

"A very *public* room. And we don't want to see it."

"I think she's jealous," Gabe said in Brianna's ear.

Brianna giggled, but her friend's narrowed eyes made her stop. "Sorry," she said, still trying to contain her laughter. "What did you need, Greer?"

"I'm summoning my grandmother tonight." Her eyes moved to Gabe. "*Please* remember to be nice so she won't turn you into a frog, or worse."

"I'll be on my best behavior." He crossed his heart with the tip of his finger.

"Meet me in the courtyard tonight." She glanced at Brianna. "Try to keep him on a leash."

"Ooo.... Kinky," he said, laughing when Greer shook her head and walked away.

"You shouldn't tease her so much," Brianna chuckled.

"I shouldn't, but I need to." He shuddered. "I need to get it out of my system before facing Hecate."

She tilted her head, seeing his worry. Her lips twitched into a smile. "You're afraid of her."

"From what I've heard of her, you will be, too."

"What do you mean?"

His lips lifted into a smile. "If all the rumors are true...Well, you'll see, Goddess."

Her stomach flipped as she wondered what kind of goddess could terrify a big, scary dragon?

Chapter Twenty-Two

The darkness would have been blinding if not for the candles surrounding the field that stretched to a wall separating the forest from the school. Greer stood in the center with Gabe, Skyler, Death and Brianna standing at the points she indicated.

Greer raised her hands and glanced toward the sky. "*Ego filii tui vel neptis, suppliciter invocare numen auxilio magicae nobis.*" (I, your granddaughter, humbly call the goddess of magic.)

The wind whipped around her, pushing against them and causing the fire from the candles to flicker as Greer continued. "*Veni ad me! Hecate! Veni ad me!*" (Come to me, Hecate!)

The wind died, silence surrounded them. For a moment, Brianna thought Greer's summoning of her grandmother hadn't worked as silence surrounded them.

"So much theatrics." A woman appeared in the center of the circle.

Brianna's eyes widened as she took in a woman dressed in a black robe with hair so black it blended with the garment. Her silver eyes reminded Brianna of the moon. She was beautiful in a dark way, but she pulsed with so much energy it frightened her.

"Next time, granddaughter, simply say my name." The goddess rolled her eyes. "There's no need for all of this..." She gestured around with her hands. "Not for you." She smiled and stepped up to Greer, cupping her cheek and gazing at her with so much love that Brianna couldn't understand why people feared her. "But you like performing spells, don't you?" Brianna heard the pride in her voice. "I see there is quite a bit of me in you."

Greer smiled as Hecate kissed her forehead, then turned to Death, tilting her head. "Death, it's been a long time."

He nodded once. "It has Hecate," he said politely.

Her lips twitched. "Persephone and Hades informed me of your love's return."

His lips lifted in a smile. "She has."

She raised her brow. "That's good."

She turned toward Skyler. "Wolf." Her lips twitched. "I have a fondness for your kind."

Then, her eyes landed on Gabe, and everyone held their breath because they understood her politeness would end with one sarcastic word. He bowed his head in greeting but seemed to struggle for words.

"You may refer to me as Hecate." She pushed out an exasperated breath. "I wouldn't want to take your pet name for your mate."

He sighed in relief. "Thank you, Hecate."

Her lips twitched. "Loyalty is admirable, and I see you have a great deal of that, especially toward her. Most would be surprised to find that in your kind, but I am not. Also, contrary to popular belief, I will not turn you into a frog...Or worse, for showing that wonderful spark. I have a sense of humor."

Gabe's shoulders relaxed. "Thank bloody hell," he breathed.

Brianna's mouth dropped open as she touched his nose with her fingertip and stepped toward her. "I am usually surprised to be summoned to aid a goddess of love, but you are more than that, aren't you?"

Brianna nodded. "Yes, Goddess."

Hecate's silver eyes slid over her. "Yet you don't have your grandfather, Ares' often abrasive nature when dealing with other gods." She smirked. "I am glad you didn't accept Persephone's gifts. We don't need you to create flowers wherever you go. Though it may have balanced you out a bit more."

Brianna frowned. All she could remember of Persephone was that she was the Queen of the Underworld.

Hecate's lips twitched. "I see you have a way to go in your studies. But you will learn. Persephone is also a goddess of the Spring." She raised her brow. "I am curious. What do you need from me?"

"Grandmother, we hope to seek your advice." Greer shifted. "As you undoubtably know, Brianna accidentally accepted most of her titles and that puts her in a certain amount of danger."

Hecate frowned, her eyes moving to Brianna, then Gabe. "Well, she is married. She could easily give him some of her gifts and make him a god. Zeus has accepted the marriage. There would be no argument from him."

Brianna fidgeted, twisting her hands in front of her as her cheeks reddened. "Well...The marriage was also an accident."

Hecate shifted her gaze from Gabe to Brianna. "Accidents aren't always mistakes."

"I agree. I would never view my bond with Gabe as a mistake, accident or not." Gabe's eyes shifted toward her. A frown marred her brow. "But I'm not ready to..."

Hecate's grin widened as mischief sparked in her moon-like eyes. "Are you certain? It is quite fun."

Brianna's face reddened further. "I-I'm sure."

Hecate's lips pressed together. "You are an odd addition to Aphrodite's line, but I respect it. I love that you are unique. Great things will come from that."

She sighed, rubbing her delicate fingers over her brow. "However, I can't make him a god, even for your protection." She dropped her hand as a grin slid over her face once more. "But I can give him some gifts that would appear as if you *did* give into his...manly charms."

Brianna blew out a breath. "Thank you."

Hecate stretched out her hand. "Come to me, Dragon."

Gabe took a deep breath and walked toward her, stopping in front of her. He shifted nervously.

Her eyes bore into his. "Do you truly care for her?"

Gabe glanced at Brianna over his shoulder. His gaze softened, causing her heart to thrum against her ribs. "Yes."

"Brave to admit it," she said, nodding. "Bravery is something given in war. Though she will retain her gifts from Ares, I think it is suited for you to have similar gifts. You'll receive strength, battle strategy, and the ability to use any weapon. Your body will glow when using these gifts."

She placed her hand on his forehead. A golden mist swirled around him, Hecate's eyes glowing white, before the golden light burst outward and faded.

"Be careful with these gifts," she warned. "Learn how to use them properly. They can be extremely dangerous if you don't."

Gabe nodded. "I will, Hecate."

She moved toward Brianna once more, taking her hands in hers. Brianna flinched at the power pulsing from Hecate's grip, buzzing against her skin. "Your mother is my friend." She glanced at Death. "As is your father. I know their history with Hera, but listen to her when she makes her decision about your marriage. She has her reasons, and they may not be what you expect."

Brianna nodded. "I will, Goddess," she whispered.

Hecate turned and stopped in front of Greer. She placed a kiss on her forehead. "Beckon me anytime you need me." Then she was gone, leaving a prickly sensation over Brianna's skin that she could only describe as magic.

BRIANNA WAS QUIET AS they headed back to their dorm. Gabe glanced at her as his brow furrowed, trying to discover what was on her mind.

"I would love to be privy to your thoughts, Goddess." He tilted his head as his eyes roamed over her face.

Brianna frowned. "Just pondering over what Hecate said to me about Hera."

Gabe's lips tilted in a smile. "Are you worried you're to be hitched to me forever?"

"Maybe you should worry about being hitched to *me*." She laughed to brighten the mood.

The truth was, the marriage to Gabe wouldn't be so daunting if they had gotten to this point normally. They went from acquaintances to married in a matter of days. She wanted what happened in between the friendship stage and the marriage stage. She supposed it was silly, but it was what she was missing.

Gabe turned and faced her, allowing the others to walk ahead of them. His eyes filled with affection. "I'm not."

She blinked, taking in his honest expression. "You're not what?"

"I'm not worried about being married to you forever." He sighed. "Perhaps I should be...I mean, I realize it's something that would be normal to be upset about...but I'm not."

"Why, though?" She asked, studying him carefully. "You barely know me."

He smiled sadly. "I know you more than I knew Neva." he said, shrugging. "But I want to know why it bothers *you*."

His face tensed and she could tell that he believed she was going to reject any feelings for him whatsoever. Her heart ached because the fact remained. He didn't believe he was good enough.

"I guess it's because I value the things in between...I want to be your friend and your girlfriend...Go out on dates and hold hands. Then, if we haven't killed each other and we want to get married, I want the ring, the question and the knee."

Gabe grinned, his eyes twinkling. "You would want to be my girlfriend?"

Brianna's cheeks reddened. "Well, I'm already your wife."

"You became my wife by accident, Goddess." His lips twitched. "Being my girlfriend would be your choice. It means more."

She gnawed on her bottom lip. "I-I would want that."

He wrapped his arm around her waist and pulled her body against his. His heart thrummed so hard, she could feel it pounding where her chest was flush against his.

He caressed her cheek as he peered into her eyes. "You would have chosen me?"

His gaze heated, and she shivered. "Yes."

He inhaled sharply just before his lips met hers. She wrapped her arms around his neck, deepening the kiss. He pulled her bottom lip between his teeth and sucked on it, causing pleasure to shoot through every nerve in her body before breaking from the kiss to rest his forehead against hers.

His breathing was ragged as he peered into her eyes with so much affection that her body trembled. "No matter the label...Call me whatever you want, Goddess whether that is guardian, boyfriend or husband...They mean the same to me because regardless, I am yours."

He kissed her again, claiming her heart a little more with every brush of his lips.

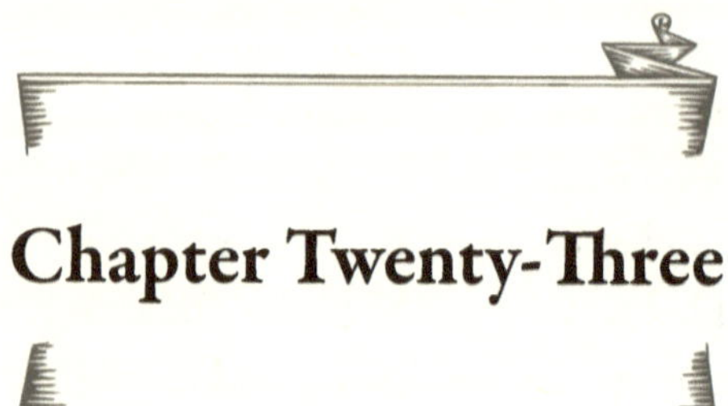

Chapter Twenty-Three

Brianna yawned as she tried to focus on the Mythology book in front of her before giving up and slamming it closed. Gabe came out of the bathroom, towel wrapped around his waist, his body glistening from his shower. For once, his normally pale skin was almost pink from the heat of the water.

When he walked up, she placed her hand on his chest and frowned. It was odd to feel the heat on his skin when it was usually cool to the touch.

He raised a brow at her, his lips twitching into a wicked grin. "What are you doing, Goddess?"

"You're warm." Her brow remained furrowed as her fingers danced over his skin.

"Momentarily. I'll be cool as ice in a few minutes."

"It's odd to feel your skin like this," she whispered.

Gabe's eyes darkened. "Would you like me better if I were warm?"

Brianna shook her head, realizing it often bothered him. "As strange as it sounds, no. I find comfort in your coolness. I prefer it to the heat."

Gabe's features relaxed as he put his hand over hers, pulling it to rest over his heart. "Good to know you would have never preferred my brother to me."

She rolled her eyes. "No matter the skin temperature."

"Has my temperature ever bothered you?" He asked, studying her face with an intensity that made her shift. "I mean...Even before you found out I was your guardian?"

She shrugged. "We barely touched."

"We sparred, and I held you after learning of Boyd's death." He frowned. "I suppose my body temperature may have been close to normal for a human during the sparring, but not when I was comforting you. You didn't feel any discomfort then?"

She shook her head. "No...I mean...I know that your skin is cool," she said and then blushed. "And I know your kiss is cold, but it's never bothered me. It's simply something I think of when I think of you. It's almost sentimental."

"That's odd." His eyes flashed with knowledge she didn't understand as he looked up and then smiled.

"Why is that odd?" she asked, frowning.

"Well, the reason why I was with Neva was she was the only female ice dragon who was my age. Ice dragons are usually only comfortable with other ice dragons because of the temperature of their skin. We pretty much recognized that either we had to be together or risk being alone."

Brianna shook her head. "But she was with Aidan."

"That's the oddity." He shook his head. "Fire dragons can adapt their temperatures because of their connections to angels. Ice dragons cannot because our fathers are fallen. Usually, fire dragons don't choose ice dragons because they can never have children together and also, they run the risk of their angel parents turning their backs on them."

"Maybe that's what I'm doing, adapting." Brianna shrugged. "I *am* a goddess."

"But you wouldn't." A smile broke out across his face. "Unless a certain line of goddesses gave you that gift because they realized we would be together. They would have seen it in the cloth. Meaning Clotho spun our lives together with the same thread."

"Wait..." She held up a hand. "What certain line of goddesses are you talking about?"

"Aphrodite's."

"And why would Clotho spin our lives together?" she asked, shaking her head.

Gabe chuckled. "Because Clotho is one of the fates and as such, she spun our lives together, because we weren't chosen for each other by chance. Everything that has brought us together has been destined, and if we were destined, the gods have had a hand in what has happened."

"Why would they do that?" Brianna asked, confused.

"I don't know." He took her hand in his. "But I think it's time we found out."

Brianna's stomach twisted. Every time she asked a new question and every time, she discovered something new about her life, it put her and those around her in danger.

WHEN APHRODITE APPEARED, she was dressed in a white, Grecian style dress. Her blonde hair flowed past her shoulders in soft waves. Roses and baby's breath were braided into the strands. Her blue eyes regarded them with a wariness that hinted she realized why she had been summoned.

"Mrs. Galatas," Brianna said, shifting slightly.

Her full lips twitched. "You can call me Aphrodite in the privacy of this room...Or grandmother."

Brianna winced as she took in Aphrodite's young appearance. She really appeared no more than twenty-five years old. "I think Aphrodite will do."

"You will get used to the gods' youthful appearances, Brianna," she said softly. "There are many of us who will not put on the mask of aging. I certainly never will."

"I'm thankful my mother and father did," she admitted. "It would have been awkward to have my parents appear only a few years older than myself."

Aphrodite laughed as she stepped forward and cupped Brianna's cheek. "You remind me so much of Juliette. She never liked my young appearance either." She sighed. "But you didn't call me here to talk about your mother or our aging processes, did you?"

"No," Brianna swallowed. "We called you here to ask about our cloths."

"Ahhh...Your cloths of life." She smiled. "I was wondering how long it would take to notice how odd your comfort was around your guardian."

"So, you do know about them?" Gabe asked.

Aphrodite rolled her eyes and studied her nails. "I not only know about them, but I've seen them. My assistance was required for your particular cloths."

Gabe narrowed his eyes. "Come off it, Aphrodite. Quit stalling. Tell us why your assistance was needed."

"If you think hard enough, you'll derive the answer." She smiled, her eyes meeting Gabe's.

"Soulmates," Gabe said, glancing from Aphrodite to Brianna.

"Soulmates?" Brianna's eyes widened. "Soulmates are real?"

"It's in the book, pumpkin. All beings once started as twin souls before Zeus cut them in two. Later, it was easier for souls to choose their mates in the abyss where all souls are made. They search until they find their mate in the darkness. They become twin souls." Gabe ran his hand through his hair, causing the almost white strands to stick up as he faced Brianna.

"You're saying our souls are twin souls?" Brianna glanced from Gabe to Aphrodite.

Aphrodite nodded, chuckling. "There was always a reason why you were my favorite dragon." She gave him a wink. "It certainly wasn't your charming personality."

"Wait," Brianna said, putting her hand out. "Does this mean we're destined to be together?"

"There is still free will and Clotho will weave your cloth according to your actions to document your life. However, your soulmate will always remain tethered to you. It's an unbreakable bond. Those who ignore the partnership of the souls hurt themselves. They always feel as if they are missing a piece in their life, even when they are at their happiest. My advice is not to fight it."

"But Aphrodite's line rarely has soulmates." Gabe shook his head. "Their powers rarely allow it."

"That's why I was surprised when I was called for Brianna, especially after being called for her mother. Usually, generations pass before that happens, but there is something special about Juliette and her children." She glanced at Brianna with her brow raised. "I was summoned because Gabe's soul cried for yours at creation and I believed he would be alone in that...until your soul cried out for his. I would put all the blame on your mother, but I also suspect Hades and Persephone's bloodline has something to do with it, too."

"Why?" Brianna asked, pursing her lips.

"Do you know their story?" Aphrodite laughed, her eyes sparkling with mischief.

"Didn't he kidnap her?" Brianna asked, terrified.

Aphrodite's mouth dropped open in immediate defense of them. "Only because Demeter tried to hide her away and break the bond." She shook her head. "I may have dropped a hint or two of where she was to Hades."

"But he kidnapped her." Brianna insisted.

"Call it Stockholm Syndrome, but she does love him," she said with a shrug of her dainty shoulder. "She's loved him from the beginning, much to her mother's dismay. But we all love our bad boys, don't we?" Aphrodite's eyes shifted to Gabe before taking on a faraway look and sighing. She turned her attention back to Brianna. "The point is, their souls cried out for each other at their creations, too, and they are happy and in love. The perfect match."

"But there is always a reason," Gabe said. "We were created that way for a purpose. Just like Persephone and Hades were created to be the King and Queen of the Underworld."

"I suppose so," she said, pursing her lips and tapping a pink-tipped nail against her chin. "I assume it's something big, but Clotho hasn't gotten to that part of the cloth yet. I simply know that I can't wait to see it. It will be a masterpiece."

"It sounds like the choice of who we are destined to be with was taken out of our hands," Brianna sighed.

Aphrodite cupped her cheeks again. Her eyes sparkled merrily. "There is always a choice," she said, "And *you* made that choice...Not the gods but *you*. At Gabe's creation, his soul cried out for you into the chaos of the abyss. It could have been a one-sided cry, but at the moment of your creation, your soul chose him. I don't know why your souls chose each other. I am not in charge of that. However, until you found each other, your souls continued to cry, but now they are silent. You are bound...There is no one who can break it, but more importantly, you are the calm to each other's storms. In that, you will find the greatest achievements, the greatest sacrifices, the greatest love."

Aphrodite kissed Brianna's forehead and backed away. "I have nothing else to offer. I must leave now," she sighed. "If I ever find the reason why your souls were matched, I will tell you." Then she faded away.

Gabe moved closer to Brianna, his brows furrowed. "I know it's a lot to take in, Goddess." He swallowed. "But it doesn't change anything for me. I have always chosen you with every breath I have taken, even the first one."

Brianna reached up and cupped his cheek, her eyes meeting his. "And I choose you, Gabe. I suppose I have from the moment of my existence."

As his lips touched her, Brianna felt her heart leap as if trying to get closer to him. She wondered if it was truly her heart, or perhaps it was her soul craving his.

Chapter Twenty-Four

Brianna's eyes drifted shut as she lay in the coolness of Gabe's arms with his lips pressed against the back of her head. A sigh escaped her as the darkness of sleep flowed through her.

A bright light on her eyelids awoke her.

A great dragon stood in front of her. Her mouth dropped open as she took in his red-scaled features. A woman with long, dark hair stood beside him, allowing his snout to nuzzle her hand, lovingly.

She was clothed in a Grecian gown that draped over her in a way that was almost regal, a golden ivy crown on her head.

"Hello, Brianna," the woman said in a voice that was both soft and rippled with power. Her silver gaze met hers and she dropped her hand from the dragon's snout. "You don't know who I am?" she asked with a smile. "There are plenty of clues here."

Brianna's gaze moved around the area. A beautiful apple orchard stretched before her containing gold, silver, red, blue, purple, yellow and green apples. Baskets sat beneath the trees on lush green grass, awaiting their harvest. Golden butterflies flew around them, leaving trails of mist in their wakes.

Brianna's gaze moved back to the woman as her eyes widened. "Hera?"

"I'm glad you've been studying." She took a step toward her. "It would have been awkward otherwise."

"I think everyone has heard of you," Brianna said softly. "Even those who are not part of the mythos."

"I was worried that you had only heard about my jealous debacles." She sighed, her expression darkening. *"Over the centuries, I have learned to control myself better."*

Brianna blushed because she had heard of Hera's jealousy. Still, she knew of other things, too. *"I've read about your grove."* She glanced at the dragon behind Hera, remembering how her guardian had been a warning to all dragons who fell in love with a god or goddess. *"And of your guardian, Ladon."*

Hera gave her a wicked grin. *"I'm sure your mother and Aphrodite have told you some less than pleasant things about me."*

Brianna winced. *"Some,"* she said, knowing it was better not to piss off the Queen of the Gods but she couldn't bite her tongue and refused to lie. *"You kept my parents from marrying."*

Hera's smile faltered. *"Something I shouldn't have done."* She glanced at the grove behind her. *"Can you walk with me?"*

Brianna gave her a wary glance, then straightened her spine, realizing it could be hazardous to her health if she refused. *"Yes, Goddess."* She gave her a tight smile. *"I'll walk with you."*

Hera held out her hand, but Brianna raised her brow, staring at it as if it were a snake. *"I won't bite."*

Brianna took a deep breath and took her warm hand in hers.

Hera smiled. *"Thank you for your company."*

"But my company is for a reason, isn't it?" Brianna pursed her lips.

"It is," Hera whispered, glancing over her shoulder where Ladon stood guard, his dark eyes following her every move. *"You see, I made a mistake, a long time ago and I need to make amends."*

Brianna turned toward her, studying her face. *"A mistake?"*

"I made a decision a long time ago to not allow a couple to marry." She blew out a breath. *"It was a form of revenge with lasting consequences."*

"My parents?" Brianna asked, raising her brows immediately suspicious of Hera's reason for appearing while she slept. *"Why didn't you allow them to marry?"*

Hera's eyes darkened. "Aphrodite was to stay married to my son, Hephaestus." She frowned. "She didn't, and I felt as if she were rejecting him based on her ideas of beauty before running to Ares' bed. She had others, too, but for some reason, Ares holds her heart. Neither has been faithful to the other. They never will be, except in their hearts. It's not in their nature."

"I still don't understand," Brianna whispered. "Why punish my mother and father?"

"I was angry at having my son tossed aside. I realize how that sounds, but that is the reason. In time, I have realized that Aphrodite does care for Hephaestus as a friend. In fact, he's her best friend. Add in the fact that he's in love with one of the Graces, Aglaea, and she returns that love, it is silly to continue with that anger. Hephaestus has moved on and has even remarried, but it took me centuries to let it go. By the time I did, the damage was done in more ways than one. The truth is that it was wrong of me to push Aphrodite and Hephaestus together, and it was wrong to punish Aphrodite and your mother. Now that I have, the balance your mother and father's marriage would have brought to the world is unbalanced and I must right the wrong, which I did at your birth."

"What do you mean, balance?" Brianna frowned.

"When soulmates are united, they balance the world. They get rid of something that was unbalanced. You and Gabe will take Juliette and Death's place and balance what they weren't able to." Hera said, her eyes wide.

"You're the one who made Gabe and me soulmates?" Brianna asked, narrowing her eyes.

"No, I am not," she raised her brow. "Your souls chose each other. However, I promised if ever given a chance to approve your marriage, I would agree to it. Of course, Zeus knew this. That was why he accepted it as soon as it was requested."

"You realize it's for only a year and a day?" Brianna asked, hoping the goddess wouldn't deny it.

"On the day your marriage hits the year and a day mark, if you ask that day to annul your marriage, I am required to accept the annulment." Her jaw tensed. *"But I ask that you both reconsider. You're meant to be with each other. Why fight it?"*

"Because I want the things before marriage," Brianna said. *"I want him to choose me. You must understand that."*

"But I don't, my dear. Both of you have already chosen." She shook her head. *"But all I'm asking is a chance to rethink your decision. That's all I want."*

Brianna tilted her head as she studied Hera. It was obviously important to her to right the wrongs of the past, and if it would end the feud between her and Brianna's family, she felt she must try.

"Okay, Goddess." Brianna gave her a small smile. *"I promise I will think about reconsidering but understand that is not a promise to stay in the marriage."*

"Fair enough." She released her hand and backed away from Brianna. "I suppose I should let you wake. Gabe is a bit distraught that you aren't heeding his calls.

Hera waved her hand in front of her and a moment later, she was staring into the panicked blue eyes of her soulmate.

"What the hell just happened?" He asked, his whole body quaking as he released a shaky breath.

"Hera happened," Brianna whispered, her voice raspy.

His eyes narrowed. "Bloody vengeful goddess," he spat out, putting his hand over his heart. "Is she trying to kill me?"

Brianna laughed, but his lips pressed together into a thin line. "No." Her lips twitched. "She's trying to keep you a married man."

His shaking stopped as his eyes took on a faraway look. Then he smiled. "In that case, go back to sleep, Goddess." He laughed. "Listen to Hera. I'll go take a shower."

He stood as she threw a pillow at him. He grinned as he reached the bathroom door. "If you aren't going to sleep, do you want to join me, wifey?"

She gripped another pillow and threw it, but it hit the closed bathroom door. She could hear his laughter from the other side. A smile slid over her face as she contemplated what life would be like if she chose to remain married to him.

AS SOON AS BRIANNA and Gabe entered the school building. Greer and Skyler rushed toward them with wide eyes. What surprised them most was Rowan standing next to them, shaking uncontrollably.

"What's the hag doing with you?" Gabe curled his lip in disgust as his eyes roamed over her.

Skyler pressed his lips together in confusion, as Greer glanced from Gabe to Rowan with a frown, struggling between her usual anger at the banshee and sympathy.

"She needs our help." Greer shook her head before staring at Rowan confused. "Though I don't understand what has happened for her to seek us out."

Taking in Rowan's tear-streaked face, Brianna's heart clenched, feeling the urge to comfort her. "Why do you need our help?"

"Goddess, you can't really mean to assist *that*!" Gabe waved his hand toward Rowan before swiping his hand over his eyes and throwing his hands up in front of him. "Of course you do. It's that sympathetic part of Aphrodite in you which keeps you from turning her away. Believe me, Goddess, you shouldn't lift a finger to assist her. She wouldn't hesitate to harm you as payment."

"I think we should listen to her." Greer shifted uncomfortably. Both Skyler and Gabe turned, their mouths falling open. If anyone should hate Rowan more than the others, it was Greer who had suffered her torment the most.

Gabe shook his head. "After everything she's done? Have you lost your mind?"

Greer shrugged, glaring at Rowan. "If she does anything...And I mean anything...I'll turn her over to my grandmother and she can decide her punishment."

Rowan paled at the mention of Hecate and burst out crying. "I swear to you, I'm not here to hurt anyone. I need help. I'm obviously desperate if I'm asking you."

"What happened?" Brianna took a step toward her, but Gabe gripped her hand, pulling her back to his side.

"You will stay by my side," Gabe ground out. "I will kill her if she touches you, then I will spank you for making me get my clothes dirty because you put yourself in danger."

Brianna rolled her eyes and turned back to Rowan. "What's happened?"

Tears streamed from her eyes as she took a deep breath. "Two of my sisters are missing. I understand why you probably assume they've gone to Kuraim, but they didn't. That's why I'm here. I know they didn't."

"How do we know you aren't one of Kuraim's minions?" Gabe asked, baring sharpened teeth.

"I'll face Alethea if that's what's needed for you to trust me," she said, trembling. "I'll allow her to see my soul."

Brianna glanced at Gabe. "Who's Alethea?"

"The goddess of truth and justice. She can see into souls and derive if they are telling the truth, but those of the mythos must allow it. Once they do, they can't lie. If they try, they die and when I say die. I mean, *they die*. Even their soul will be destroyed."

Brianna studied Rowan's face. "And you're sure you want to face her to prove you are telling the truth?"

"Yes. I realize you don't trust me, but I am telling the truth," She said, then turned, walking down the hallway without another word.

Gabe's lip curled. "I hope she doesn't think we're going to become besties."

Brianna opened her mouth to reply but the intercom crackling interrupted her. "Would Brianna Isolde, Gabriel Isolde, Skyler Sheldon, and Greer Newton come to the office?"

Gabe groaned. "Bloody hell," he whispered, running his hands through his hair. When Brianna glanced at him, her eyes were wide. His dragon was flashing, becoming darker and darker beneath his skin, but more than that, he was glowing gold.

"You need to calm down," she said, her brows raised.

"Why is that, Goddess?" He asked, his hands curled into fists.

Her eyes slid over him, realizing anyone who was around him would immediately see he was upset. "Hecate's gift to you worked," she said. "You're glowing."

He glanced down at himself and took a deep breath before he spat out. "Bloody...Fucking...Fantastic."

Brianna frowned, wondering why Rowan had been able to upset him so much as they made their way to the office. Upon opening the door, she realized this meeting would be about much more than two missing banshees as she met the eyes of the god of war.

Chapter Twenty-Five

A res' almost seven-feet tall, muscular frame filled the room with electricity that was almost palpable. His green eyes moved from Brianna to Gabe, flashing with an angry fire that shook through the air with the force of a tsunami.

"You made him a god?" His voice rumbled, making the walls quiver. "One of *my* gods of war?"

Brianna raised a brow, pressing herself against Gabe's side before narrowing her eyes. Though Ares was terrifying in his rage, she refused to back down from him. To do that would give him dominion over her. He would wield that power whether she was his granddaughter or not.

She curled her hands into fists. "I don't know who you think—"

Gabe's hand covered her mouth, pulling her against him. "Please don't piss him off, Goddess," he said into her ear. "His temper will literally start a war."

Greer stepped forward, facing the god of war, her eyes remaining steady on him. "He's not a god, but he has been given a gift that mimics someone of your bloodline." Brianna was surprised at her calmness under his feral glare. "It was given to protect Brianna." She squared her shoulders and narrowed her gaze. "So, calm down before I call Atropos to cut the thread of life on your greatest warriors."

"And why would she do that, little witch?" Ares growled.

"Because the Fates have taken an interest in Gabe and Brianna's destinies and any threat to them would be enough to really piss them off," Greer said, sweetly.

Ares frowned, but his fierce expression softened as he ran his hand through his thick, brown hair. His handsome face relaxed as his green eyes settled on Brianna and Gabe, the menacing glow within them not as bright.

"So, my granddaughter still retains my gifts?" He asked, sighing as if relieved.

Brianna frowned as Gabe removed his hand from her mouth, then tilted his head. "Wait...You weren't upset I had them, just that she would give them up?"

Brianna's mouth dropped open before she laughed. "Your feelings were hurt?"

Ares curled his lip before shrugging one of his massive shoulders. "Not hurt...Disappointed. Very few from my bloodline choose my lineage as the source of their power. Supposedly, it's volatile." A brief look of confusion crossed his face before he shook his head. "But you did choose to claim it...Even if it was by accident. I hope you will choose to keep it."

"So, you came here to ask me to keep my gifts from your line?" Brianna asked, frowning.

"Yes. Aphrodite said it was best to have a discussion instead of keeping my worries to myself." Brianna smiled as his expression became almost tender. She realized Aphrodite balanced Ares, and she was sure in some ways he balanced her. "But I also came to help my granddaughter." He glanced at Gabe. "And not simply by giving her instructions during battle." He coughed over the tenderness, straightening his spine. "I think I know where Kuraim is, as well as his next move. If I'm right, you'll need an army before you face him. I'm here to offer my military to you."

Brianna glanced at Gabe, who nodded. A smile slid across her face as she stepped toward Ares, tilting her head back to stare into his eyes.

"It's nice to meet you, grandfather," she said, warmed by the fact that he wanted to help her.

ARES MOTIONED FOR THEM to sit down with the sweep of one of his massive hands. His towering frame cast a shadow over them as he leaned against Mr. Leo's desk, crossing his arms over his chest.

"First, we should talk about the students who came up missing last night." His jaw clenched as he glanced at each of them. "Banshees, mermaids, gorgons, witches, and werewolves are all missing...And not just here, but throughout the mythos world and the cities and towns beyond this school."

Brianna and Greer exchanged a look before turning back to Ares. "A banshee...Rowan asked us for help this morning," Brianna said, frowning. "Her sisters are missing."

"Do you think they went to Kuraim?" Gabe asked Ares, but he shook his head.

"No, though I don't think they fared well." He shifted. "Death isn't here because of a number of bodies that have been found without their souls. So far, we haven't found banshees, but if Rowan and the rest of the banshees are willing to assist us, it will help a great deal. Banshees are great warriors."

"She's offered to meet Alethea to prove we can trust her," Gabe said, his gaze darkening.

Ares nodded. "Then allow her to do so." He rolled his muscled shoulders. "At least we will find out if she's on our side. She won't be able to lie to Alethea...Not without dying."

"You said you know where Kuraim is..." Brianna uttered, her stomach churning with the possibility of facing the being who had ordered Boyd's death and had killed the Oracle.

"Yes, though it is not a good idea to meet him there." Ares squinted as if he were calculating something in his head.

"Why not?" Gabe asked, tensing beside Brianna. "If we don't confront him now, we may lose him."

"It's too risky. He's in Atlantis and considering I've heard the prophecies, I don't want to put either my granddaughter or her guardian in danger." He raised his brows. "An island with no escape is not the ideal place to wage this battle. Besides, Kuraim and his followers are preparing to come here."

Gabe sucked in a breath.

"How do you know that?" Brianna asked.

Ares smirked. "The same way any good warlord knows. I planted a spy."

Brianna's eyes widened. "Who?"

"You'll find that out when the time is right." His lips twitched. "For now, I struck a deal with Zeus to protect you and Gabe. I'm privy to the prophecies that seemed to predict one of your deaths. Let's make that harder to achieve."

"How are you going to do that?" Gabe asked, crossing his arms over his chest.

"One of the reasons Brianna never suspected she was a goddess is that Julie and Death decided it was best for her to have her gifts blocked. They are still somewhat inactive. They will reach their full power when she's twenty, but as you can see, that is too long to wait. So, Zeus has agreed to activate Brianna's gifts, so she will now be a goddess in truth. Her human body will strengthen and become immortal. She will be much harder to kill." He eyed Gabe. "And Zeus has agreed to make you the god of dragons, which means you will become one of my warrior gods. That is, if you accept it."

Brianna furrowed her brows, confused. "But I thought only a...bond with a god or goddess could create gods."

Ares shook his head. "No, as the king of the gods, Zeus has always been able to appoint any being as a god or goddess. He simply hasn't done so in centuries. Most have forgotten he has the ability."

"Forgive me, but I must remind you that my father is a fallen." Gabe's shoulders fell forward. "Why would Zeus choose to do this for me? No child of a fallen has ever become a god."

"You're right. This will be a first for Olympus." Ares eyes bore into Gabe's. "However, you've proven you are nothing like your mother nor your father., and we learn from our mistakes. For example, I once denied my daughter a marriage because of the lineage of a truly great man. I listened to Hera, wanting her praise, her acceptance. I won't make that mistake again. However, you have work to do yourself. You must accept that your lineage means nothing when it comes to your character and realize their sins are not yours. You have to see yourself as worthy. Can you do that to protect yourself, but also Brianna?"

Gabe glanced at Brianna, his gaze softening, and nodded his head. "I will do anything to protect her."

Ares patted him on the shoulder. "Then we go in the morning to meet with Zeus." He glanced at Brianna, his eyes sparkling with excitement. "Call Alethea tonight to test the banshee but then prepare to go to the home of the gods...Mount Olympus."

Chapter Twenty-Six

Rowan was silent as she followed Greer, Skyler, Brianna and Gabe. Gabe glanced over his shoulder, narrowing his eyes at the banshee, his mistrust clear on his face.

When Brianna followed his gaze, her eyes widened as she found that Rowan's hair was streaked with gray.

"What is wrong with her hair?" Brianna whispered to Gabe.

Gabe's upper lip curled in disgust. "Perhaps she's upset over her sister's disappearance," he said, then raised his voice so Rowan could hear. "Or perhaps she's been a part of Kuraim's militia the whole time."

Brianna heard Rowan sigh. Her gaze moved over Gabe's face. "You really don't trust her, do you?"

Gabe ground his teeth, the edges becoming sharper as his dragon flashed beneath his skin. A gold mist glowed around his body. "Of course not. When I first arrived, she tried to get me expelled for almost freezing her, but it was her fault. Everybody in the mythos knows you don't enter an ice dragon's bedroom and wake him with that awful howl. But then, she did something worse."

Brianna frowned. "What's that?"

Gabe's lips twitched into a smile, flashing his teeth. "She messed with my goddess." He raised a brow. "You have no *idea* how much I wanted to turn her to ice for that little trick she played on you."

"I'm okay now." She shrugged but remembered how truly terrifying the ordeal had been.

"Doesn't matter, Goddess." He leaned down to whisper in her ear, the ice from his breath coating her skin. "No one harms you without expecting retribution."

Brianna's lips curled into a smile. Gabe had been protective of her from the beginning. She had simply failed to notice. She leaned into him, gripping his hand in her own as they made their way into the field where Greer had called upon Hecate.

"Bloody hell," Gabe mumbled, taking in the field before running his hand through his hair, causing it to spike in all directions. "I guess I'll have to be on my best behavior again."

Brianna's gaze moved to the field, her eyes going wide as she took in the gods standing around the circle. She recognized Hecate in the center. Aphrodite stood to the east, Juliette to the west, Ares had taken his place to the south and Death stood to the north. Candles flickered around them as they raised their hands.

"What are they doing?" Brianna whispered.

Greer crossed her arms over her chest, pouting. "Grandmother said I was too young to call upon Alethea, so they gathered to call her for the test."

Brianna smiled at Greer, hoping to give her some comfort. Greer sulked toward the circle with a sigh as Alethea's name rose through the air as a blast of gray light expanded over the circle. Brianna blinked, surprised, when a beautiful goddess dressed in a gray Grecian dress stood in the middle beside Hecate. Her eyes were so glazed and so silver, they reflected the world around her. Her white hair blew around her flawless face.

"Why was her light gray?" Brianna asked, wondering at the lack of color.

Greer smiled, sadly. "Because justice is neither black nor white. In justice, there is always a victim and an abuser. Both are affected. Regardless of who is considered right, there are no winners. In the end, both lose something."

Brianna's heart clenched as she took in Alethea's face. No smile rested upon it, and as her gaze moved around the circle, she realized she wasn't truly seeing it.

"Is Alethea blind?" Brianna asked, frowning as her chest constricted.

"Justice is blind," Gabe uttered. "She is the reason for that saying."

"But why?" Enthralled, Brianna stepped closer to the circle.

"Because sometimes you have to be blind to truly see into a being's soul." Greer took an athame from her belt and walked toward the circle, leading Rowan toward it with Skyler following behind her, in case she tried to run.

Gabe turned to Brianna. "Do you want to stay?" He asked, glancing at the circle with a worried frown. "If she is lying, she will die. Her death won't be pretty. I'm not sure such a scene will be fit for your pretty eyes."

Brianna nodded, though her stomach churned. "I need to know if she has told the truth." She shifted. "I need to know if she's trustworthy."

"Goddess, no matter if she passes Alethea's test, Rowan will *never* be trustworthy." He glared at Rowan with narrowed eyes. "I've watched her over the years. Not once has she shown kindness unless it benefitted herself."

Brianna gave him a sad smile. "I believe people can change. Maybe this ordeal will help her do that."

His eyes widened, and he became very still before a smile crossed his face. He leaned forward and kissed her forehead. "Perhaps you're right."

Alethea's ghost-like whisper rippled through the air as she called Rowan's name, causing both Gabe and Brianna to turn.

"Oh my..." Brianna breathed as she took in the Goddess facing Rowan. Alethea's pale hands clutched each of the banshee's cheeks as her sightless, silver eyes peered into Rowan's. The surface of Alethea's eyes rippled like water before stilling. A scream echoed from between Rowan's lips, causing the world to shake around them as they covered their ears. Finally, her screams stopped.

"Does that mean she's lying?" Brianna asked, but Gabe shook his head.

"Alethea shows them their sins before justice is served." Alethea released Rowan. Tears streaked the banshee's face. "It's excruciating."

"Hecate, ask the questions for which you seek answers," Alethea said in that wavering whisper. "Rowan shall answer them truthfully or face the true death."

Hecate turned to Rowan. "Do you wish harm to anyone at this school?"

Rowan's bottom lip trembled. "Yes."

Brianna straightened as a gust of wind whipped around the circle.

"Truth," Alethea sighed.

Gabe pulled Brianna closer to him as Hecate spoke again. "Who do you wish harm?"

Rowan raised her chin. "Greer."

The wind whipped around the circle. "Truth," Alethea whispered.

Greer groaned. "Of course it's me."

"Why do you wish her harm?" Hecate asked, raising her brow.

"Because I believed that Aidan cared about her," she said, her hair streaking white as she spoke.

"She's out of her mind," Greer said, her brow furrowing, but Alethea confirmed that Rowan's answer was honest.

Hecate spoke again. "Are you in league with Kuraim?"

"No," Rowan answered breathlessly, her hands clutching her chest.

"Truth," Alethea said.

Hecate spoke again. "Do you plan to join him?"

Rowan shook her head. "No."

Another gust of wind as Alethea whispered, "Truth."

Hecate tilted her head. "Do you know where your sisters are?"

Chapter Twenty-Seven

Gabe's muscles were rigid as his eyes narrowed. A glaze of ice settled on Brianna's skin from the cold he emitted. She could sense the sheer power of his dragon itching to attack. Athena raised a brow, stepping away from him.

"What's wrong?" Brianna whispered, frowning, as the others stepped away from them.

"Medusa," he growled as the only explanation, his teeth sharpened into fangs.

Brianna's eyes widened as she remembered the story of Medusa from her mythology book. The gorgon's likeness was displayed all over the school, but Medusa's story wasn't heroic. Instead, it was tragic. Poseidon had raped her in Athena's temple and in the goddess' fury, Athena turned her into a gorgon. Then Perseus had killed her by beheading her. Being cursed as a gorgon was now used for those who were intimate with a fallen...like Gabe's mother. Their children were turned into dragon shifters.

"Calm, dragon," Athena said, softly. Her eyes sliding over him, taking in his weaknesses in a moment in case they needed to battle. "I'm not here to harm you. I'm here to help you."

Hecate joined them, her silver gaze moving from Gabe to Athena but remaining silent.

"Forgive me if I would bet on Zeus keeping it in his pants before I would trust that you would want to help me," Gabe said, his eyes hard as his monster flashed beneath his skin yet again.

Athena's face remained calm. "Then allow me to prove it. After all, many have changed their opinions about *you*."

Gabe's nostrils flared, puffs of icy mist blowing from them. "The difference between you and me is I didn't actually do the deeds they believed me capable of. You did."

Athena straightened, her eyes remaining on him, flashing with remorse. "I admit, I acted in anger instead of wisdom. It remains far from my finest moment, but even I, the goddess of wisdom, can do stupid things. I can make mistakes. Surely, you can understand that and allow me to redeem myself."

"I don't trust you," he said through his teeth.

She sighed. "You don't have to. I haven't earned it...yet."

With that, she turned and walked toward the school, Gabe's icy glare on her back. Brianna gripped his hand, pulling his gaze to her. His dragon flashed. She wondered if Athena could ever gain the trust of someone who she had hurt so much.

AS THEY MADE THEIR way back to their room, Gabe's jaw remained clenched, his teeth grinding. He remained close, his coldness settled in ice droplets over her skin. He made no move to touch Brianna as he closed the door to their room, clicking the lock as he did. His dragon flashed beneath his skin as he turned, causing Brianna's heart to race as she realized she was alone with a beast.

She reached for him, hoping to calm him, but he flinched away. "I'm not safe right now, Goddess," he gritted out in a rough voice she didn't recognize as his body trembled, causing his muscles to twitch. Mist puffed out from between his lips with each breath.

She frowned, the need to comfort him greater than fear. She stepped forward, running her fingers over his jaw. His eyes closed as he inhaled deeply. "You won't hurt me," she whispered. "Not even now."

His eyes opened, flashing with such vulnerability that her heart clenched. He closed his fists at his sides, fighting against his dragon as she pressed her body against his. The coolness of his dragon sank into her skin, heating her blood as her arms slid around his neck, her eyes never leaving his as she begged him silently to allow her to help him.

Something broke in his eyes, fracturing light and ice as he bent forward and crushed his lips against hers. There was no hesitancy in his kiss. It was brazen as his teeth slid over her bottom lip. His tongue swept out, begging for entrance. A sigh escaped her lips as his tongue clashed with hers. She arched into him, his hands sliding from her waist to beneath her ass, lifting her and carrying her to their bed.

She could feel how much he desired her...Needed her as his body fell upon hers. Her breathing hitched as he pressed against her, moaning into her mouth. She pulled him closer as her stomach tensed pleasantly, kissing him back with the same fervor, wanting to lose herself in him. His breath was so cold against hers that it settled like ice upon her skin before her heat melted it. He groaned, his hands clenching in the fabric of her shirt before lifting his head and peering into her eyes.

His brow was furrowed, his teeth clenched in restraint. "Goddess?"

Somewhere in the haze of lust, she realized he was asking her permission. Her hand was still cupping the back of his neck as she peered into his eyes, wanting him in every way that she could. She tugged him forward. His lips touched hers, worshipping her mouth. His hand slid under her shirt, over the bare skin of her stomach, to cup her breast.

"Goddess, I l—"

A knock at the door stopped him from speaking further. He pulled away, staring at her, his body shaking and his teeth becoming fangs.

"Ignore them," she whispered, but his eyes shadowed as the knock came again.

"This school is full of a bunch of cockblockers," he groaned, his head falling to her chest as he tried to compose himself. Laughter bubbled from her throat as his dragon calmed and slinked back into the confines of his body. He was back to simply being Gabe.

He kissed her softly and rested his forehead against hers as her mother's voice echoed through the door.

"Later," he whispered as he moved from her, his spine straighter than normal, to answer the door.

Brianna ran her hand over her face, grinding her teeth in frustration. She glanced at her mother's knowing smile, realizing she had interrupted them on purpose. At that moment, she had never been so angry with her in her life.

"What was so important that you had to rush over here, mother?" Brianna snapped, causing Gabe to chuckle.

Juliette raised a brow. "Zeus doesn't want to wait to see you," she said, that mischievous smile sliding over her face again as she held up a Grecian style dress, then threw it at Brianna. "Get dressed. We're going to Olympus tonight."

Brianna's eyes widened as her mother turned to leave, but Juliette turned back to them with a twinkle in her eye, causing Brianna's eyes to narrow further. "Oh...And we don't have time for any hanky-panky."

Brianna's cheeks flamed as her mother walked away. Gabe's loud laughter rippled through the room as she buried her face in the pillow. Gabe was right. This place was full of nothing but cockblockers.

Chapter Twenty-Eight

Brianna stepped out of the bathroom. Gabe's eyes heated as his gaze swept from her hair flowing loose over her shoulders down her back to the white, Grecian dress that draped her body in a way that gave her an air of innocence and sensuality, to her feet clad in thong sandals. His breathing quickened as he took a step closer to her, licking his lips.

"I know I call you goddess often, but you fit the part perfectly tonight," he whispered. "You're so divine, I worry if I touch you, you'll shatter, and I'll have to face the fact you were just a beautiful illusion."

Brianna blushed and reached out, placing her hand on his bare chest, feeling his heart thumping beneath her fingertips. "I'm very real but thank you."

He covered her hand with his own, taking a deep breath as a smile twitched over his face. His eyes held so much affection that her body heated. "Then I am luckier than any god that has ever existed."

His lips met hers gently, the coolness of them sinking into her skin and heating the blood pumping through her veins. He pulled away to rest his forehead against hers. His eyes were dark with a need that she was sure matched her own. His lips parted as if to say something, but a knock sounded at the door.

"Cockblockers," he said, making her laugh as he opened the door.

Greer's gaze moved over Brianna and nodded in approval. "You definitely look like a goddess," she said, then her eyes traveled to Gabe, who only wore white dress pants and white Chucks. He walked to the closet and grabbed a white button-up shirt.

"Is that what you're wearing?"

"What did you expect me to wear? A toga?" he asked. She raised her brows. "Sorry, Greer. My manly bits are for Brianna's eyes only. I'm not going to run the risk of flashing all of Olympus, even if it would make them rethink male perfection."

Greer rolled her eyes before turning to Brianna, exasperation written across her face. "How can you put up with him?"

Brianna glanced at a smiling Gabe as he buttoned his shirt over his rippling abs. "Because he is pretty perfect to me."

Greer made a gagging sound. "Nauseating," she said, shaking her head. "Anyway, your guide is here. She's waiting in my room."

"Guide?" Brianna frowned, glancing toward the door. "I thought my mother or father would be accompanying us to Olympus."

Greer shook her head, causing her brown curls to brush against her cheeks. "Your parents and grandparents were called to a meeting with the Fates." She smiled. "Your cousin, a goddess of love and sexuality, will guide you."

Brianna's brows raised. "My cousin? I have cousins?"

"Many, as well as aunts and uncles." She blew out a breath. "You really should study more. This one is Eros' and Psyche's daughter, Catareena. She's really excited to meet you. So, you should hurry."

Gabe moved beside Brianna as he finished tucking his shirt in his pants. "I'm ready when you are, Goddess."

She turned toward him, her eyes widening as her mouth suddenly went dry. In all white, Gabe resembled an angel...A really hot angel.

He wrapped an arm around her waist and leaned toward her ear. "Like what you see, Goddess."

"Very much," she said. His icy breath touched her bare neck just before he placed a kiss on her skin, making her shiver.

"Oh, my goddess!" Greer called out, obviously to stop them. "Look at that! It's time to leave."

Brianna laughed as Gabe narrowed his eyes. "One day, Greer...One day, we will be able to repay you for your...*punctuality*."

Greer's eyes darkened. "I doubt it, Dragon," she said in a sweet voice, opening the door to her room.

"Don't doubt it, you little witch," he hissed. "One day, you will fall in love and I will knock on your door or call you every time you're alone with the poor tool."

Brianna giggled. "Me too."

He grinned as they stepped into Greer's room. A goddess with long red hair stood there. Blue-green eyes widened, sparkling with excitement as she bounced on her toes. Her beautiful face flushed red as she clapped her hands together.

"Oh cuz!" she chirped, her smile spreading across her face. "I'm so excited to finally meet you!"

Brianna grinned, dazzled by the goddess before her. She was a few inches taller than Brianna. A dress similar to her own draped her curves, giving her a sensual air that somehow complemented her innocent enthusiasm.

"It's nice to meet you," Brianna said, grinning. "If you didn't know already, I'm Brianna, and this is Gabe."

Gabe was grinning, obviously amused by this goddess. "It's a pleasure to meet you. Honestly, I'm so glad you are the one to escort us. I was worried the one they chose would—"

"Have a stick up their ass?" Catareena quipped, making Brianna and Gabe laugh.

Gabe nodded. "Exactly."

"Most of them aren't so bad once you get to know them," she shrugged. "Besides, you both will be joining us soon. You've already shaken things up. I can't wait to see what else you do." Catareena gazed into Brianna's eyes, a sparkle within them. "I'm going to be your favorite cousin."

Brianna smiled. "I have no doubt."

"But first things first." She bounced on her toes, making Brianna wonder if she was always this enthusiastic about everything. "Take a deep breath. Transporting this way can sometimes make it hard to breathe, but it's a quick trip."

Brianna inhaled, and everything swirled around them. When the world focused again, she found herself standing in a city mixed with Grecian columns and modern archways, twisting the present with the past in a beautiful array of architecture.

Brianna glanced at Gabe. His anxiety mixed with hers as Catareena turned toward them with a large smile, holding out her arms. "Welcome to Olympus, home of the Greek gods!"

Chapter Twenty-Nine

"The Kings and Queens of the Greek gods want to see you in the throne room," Catareena said, pointing toward a massive square structure in the center of the city.

"Lead the way," Gabe said, wrapping his arm around Brianna's waist. She raised her brows at him when she noticed his hand was trembling slightly, the muscles in his face tense.

"Is this really Mount Olympus?" Brianna asked, glancing at her surroundings. Her eyes widened at a building with wings engraved on the double doors.

"It is...but it's not." Catareena glanced over her shoulder. "This is the Mount Olympus that humans may refer to as a godly realm. The Mount Olympus on earth is not the same as this."

Brianna glanced around curiously. "Do people come here when they die?"

Her cousin giggled. "None of the dead reside here. Those who worship the Greek gods go to Hades upon their deaths. They are judged and dispersed to the places they have earned through how they lived their lives. Your grandfather is a just god. Sometimes, he chooses rebirth, and sometimes the realms of the Underworld. It depends upon their deeds."

"And I will meet with him today?" Brianna asked, suddenly nervous to be in the presence of the one who judged those who died.

"You'll be in the presence of four of your grandparents. Persephone, Hades, Zeus, and Hera. Of course, Zeus is also your great-grandfather, Persephone's father."

"Ew." Brianna wrinkled her nose. "Incest?"

"It happens often here," Gabe said, earning another disgusted look from her. He snorted. "You really should study. For example, Zeus, Hera, Poseidon and Demeter are all siblings. So, they are also your aunts and uncles."

Brianna winced as the thought of that took an even more sinister air. "I now have a reason *not* to study."

Gabe laughed. "Okay...Maybe not the family trees, but you really should learn the rest."

"So...How is Hera, my grandmother?" Brianna asked, not sure she wanted to know the answer.

"Zeus and Hera are Ares' parents," Catareena said, causing Brianna to blink in shock.

"But she was angry with Aphrodite and Ares because Aphrodite didn't fall for Hephaestus and fell in love with Ares instead."

"She was..." Catareena said, slowly, "but Ares isn't her favorite child."

Anger sparked in Brianna's chest as black bled around her. How dare Hera punish one child for another?

"No, Goddess," Gabe said, pulling her against his chest. "Not here."

"She denied my parents' marriage because she wanted revenge on her own son," she said through clenched teeth.

"And she's trying to fix that," he reminded her, his voice soft. "Breathe...Please. You don't want these nice gods to hurt your hubby, do you?"

The thought of Gabe hurt caused her anger to cool, and the darkness faded from around her. "Why would they hurt you?"

A smile tilted across his face. "Because I would have to protect you."

Brianna smiled as Catareena clapped, her eyes getting big. "I totally ship you two. You better last, or I'll have to give you a cosmic ass-whooping."

Brianna laughed as they walked up the steps of the throne room. Catareena turned, meeting Brianna's eyes. The usual mischief faded, replaced by concern. "Are you good now?"

Brianna nodded. Catareena's smile returned to her face as she threw open the double doors and led them in. The eyes of the Kings and Queens of the Greek gods all turned toward them.

BRIANNA'S EYES MOVED to Hera. Her anger flared again, so she shifted her gaze to the god beside her...Zeus. It was easy to see why so many women had fallen into his bed. His dark, wavy hair curled around his ears and framed his handsome face. Blue eyes, the same shade as her own, swept over her before he smiled. To his right was a god she instinctively recognized as Poseidon, his hair so dark it was almost black. His dark eyes moved over her as a sensual smile slid over his full lips. Brianna shifted closer to Gabe as her eyes moved to his wife, Amphitrite, an exquisite red-head with sea-green eyes who gave her a slight nod.

Brianna glanced at Zeus' left. Hades regarded her almost proudly. His dark blue eyes shined from a face even more handsome than Zeus'. Blond hair, the same shade as her own, swept back from his forehead in waves that reached his chin. Out of the three gods before her, she was most comfortable with Hades, which should have surprised her, but somehow, it didn't. Beside him was a petite blonde, who she realized must be Persephone, with green eyes that sparkled with an innocence that drew Brianna toward her. Warmth shined from her that enveloped Brianna in something as intimate as a hug.

Catareena stepped forward and bowed her head in each of their directions, beckoning Gabe and Brianna to do the same. They followed her example.

"Brianna, it is a pleasure to meet you," Zeus said in a powerful and deep voice. "As I'm sure all in attendance will agree."

Brianna straightened. "It is an honor to be in the presence of my family," she said, biting back the anger and saying the closest thing to the truth she could muster.

"We've called you here to assist you," Hera said, straightening when Brianna's icy gaze met hers. "I realize that you may not believe some of us, but it is the truth."

"And in that regard," Hades said, capturing her attention, "You and your mate shall be granted the gift of godship."

She narrowed her eyes at him. Out of all the gods before her, she had a feeling he would be the most truthful.

"What will you want in return?" Brianna asked. His lips twitched into a smile, displaying dimples denting each cheek.

"You're a smart girl." He chuckled. "You should always ask what is required of you before you agree to anything. All we require is the fulfillment of prophecies that will bring down Kuraim."

"We will do our best." Brianna offered him a smile.

"You will accomplish it," Zeus said. "I have no doubt."

She didn't know what to say as Zeus stood to step down the steps to the white-and-gold marble floor where Gabe, Brianna, and Catareena stood. He glanced at Catareena. "Please stay as a witness."

Catareena nodded as his hands clasped Brianna's shoulders, staring deep into her eyes. Power radiated from his touch. "You, Brianna, shall be the Goddess of the Balance of Light and Dark, as well as the Goddess of Dragons. These shall be your main titles, though you shall retain your gifts from your ancestors and be a minor goddess of those gifts, as well."

His lips touched her forehead. Her body heated as white light spread through her. She inhaled as the light faded, and the power she sensed in Zeus radiated through her.

Zeus stepped toward Gabe. "You shall be the God of Dragons, but I give you an extra title." Zeus narrowed his eyes upon him. "You shall also be the God of the Balance of Day and Night."

"Isn't that the same as Brianna's title?" Gabe asked, frowning.

Zeus laughed. "Can you have light at night?"

"Yes, King Zeus, you can."

"And you can have darkness during the day?" he asked, raising his dark brows.

"Yes."

Zeus chuckled. "It's good you realize the difference now." He frowned. "Now, take a deep breath. This may hurt an ice dragon."

Zeus touched his forehead with the tips of his finger. Immediately, light slid through Gabe. His pain-filled scream echoed through the room. Brianna sucked in a breath, lost as to how to help. But before she could move, his screams ceased, and he took a deep, shuddering breath. His tearful eyes glanced at Brianna.

"I'm okay," he whispered in a hoarse voice.

Zeus turned toward Catareena, sweeping his hand toward Brianna and Gabe. She grinned and stepped in front of them. "It is my honor to be the first to welcome the God of Dragons, the Balance of Day and Night and the Goddess of Dragons, Balance of Light and Dark, War, Death and Love to Olympus. May your greatness be legendary."

Brianna grasped Gabe's hand, sensing the power pulsing through them both. At that moment, she knew they had enough strength to win this battle.

Chapter Thirty

Hades rose from his throne, followed by Persephone. His eyes sparkled as his hands settled on Brianna's shoulders before pressing his lips to her forehead. He moved in front of Gabe and shook his hand. Persephone pulled Brianna into her arms before pulling back and cupping her cheeks.

"I'm so glad to meet you, my beautiful granddaughter," Persephone said as the scent of roses surrounded them.

Brianna smiled at the woman as her warmth and love enveloped her. "I'm glad to meet you, too."

Persephone stepped back as Catareena joined them, her eyes dark. "You have been summoned by the Fates," she said in a soft voice, her expression tense. Brianna tilted her head as she gazed upon the goddess, wondering if she was afraid. "Perhaps Hades and Persephone would like to join us?"

Persephone gazed up at her husband, affection shining from her eyes. "We would love to."

Persephone reached forward, gripping Brianna's hand. Everything spun for a moment, then cleared. When Brianna's sight straightened, she faced three beautiful dark-skinned goddesses. All were identical in every way except their eyes were different colors. The room they occupied was so large it stretched for miles, with woven tapestries displayed on the walls. White orbs of light darted through the top, which was free of a roof.

"The orbs are souls." Catareena pointed toward them, seeing Brianna's interest.

The sister to the right lifted her light blue gaze to Brianna as she pulled the thread from a hole in the table.

"I am Lachesis," she whispered softly. "Welcome, Brianna and Gabriel. It's been a while since we've been in your presence.

The one weaving the cloth raised her green eyes to them. "I am Clotho." Her voice seemed a little louder than her sister. "Your fate has led you here once again."

Brianna glanced at Gabe, confused, then gazed at the last of the sisters whose eyes were dark purple. Her voice was grim. "I am Atropos, and I shall be busy today." Her voice was so sorrowful it hurt Brianna's soul.

"Busy?" Brianna asked, dread settling in her stomach.

"Call your warriors," Clothos said, her eyes fixed on the fabric in front of her. "Call them here."

"Why?" Gabe asked.

"Souls begin here," Lachesis uttered. "All souls, including the evil ones. This is where evil was born."

Brianna blinked as a voice whispered through her mind. *From the darkness and ice comes the guardian of the daughter of Death. Suspect from first. Only his blood will heal the descendant of love and those who perish. Twin souls of light and night face the one where evil began...'*

"Where evil began..." Brianna's eyes widened as she realized what they meant and that they had been wrong to assume evil began in Mid-Veil. "Evil began here."

Gabe frowned and then darkness slid into his eyes and he knew. "The prophecy," he whispered. "Kuraim isn't attacking the school. He's preparing to come here to Olympus."

"Call your warriors," Clothos said, her expression grim. "Time runs short."

"Ares!" Gabe called out as his dragon flashed beneath his skin.

The walls trembled, then fell into the floor, leaving them in an open field on the borders of Olympus with the Fates still weaving in the center.

A flash of light moved around them as Ares and Aphrodite arrived. Ares' eyes were dark as they met their terrified gaze. His body straightened to its full height.

Hades closed his eyes. When he opened them, he pierced Ares with eyes that appeared almost black. "Call your soldiers," he said in a cold voice. "Kuraim is coming to Olympus."

As he spoke the final word, the ground began to shake.

GABE PULLED BRIANNA against his chest, wrapping his arms around her protectively. His heart thumped beneath her ear. A tremble moved through him as his body temperature dropped. He placed a finger beneath her chin and tilted her head up. His eyes had paled to such a light blue color they were almost white. Brianna could have sworn she saw the pattern of a snowflake within his gaze.

"No matter what happens, don't put yourself in danger."

"You can't ask me to do that," she choked out, tears burning her eyes.

"I'm not asking, Goddess. As your guardian, I'm telling you."

Brianna narrowed her eyes. "As your wife, I'm not going to listen."

His gaze softened as he bent and brushed his lips over hers, pouring so much affection into the soft movement that she could feel his love without him ever saying the words.

She broke the kiss, tears sliding down her face. She was determined he would not die, even if she had to give her life to protect him.

"Don't cry." He wiped the tears from her cheeks with the pads of his thumbs. "Don't show him weakness. He feeds off it."

"I'm a woman, Gabe. I'm going to cry." She straightened her spine and squared her shoulders. "But even the weakest woman fights her fiercest with tears in her eyes because that means she has something to fight for."

Despair washed over his face as voices rose around them. Death's angry voice made Brianna pull her gaze away from Gabe's, seeing warriors of all kinds within the area. Dragons, werewolves, banshees, angels and students from their school stood amongst the gods and goddesses. Her eyes landed on her friends, Greer and Skyler, as well as Sam. Mrs. Knight stood beside Leah Wells, the fire dragon who had been suspected of Boyd's death until Alona showed herself. There were more she did not recognize filling the field.

Death and Juliette stood facing each other, his face red, but his eyes darkened with fear. "You can't fight Juliette," he growled, nostrils flaring. "You haven't fought in over a decade. Go home!"

Juliette touched his cheek and the muscles in his face softened. At that moment, Brianna had no doubt that Death and Juliette loved each other. Death bent and kissed her with so much passion that Brianna's heart melted. Her parents still loved each other...Marriage or not. It was a revelation that caused her to forgive both for keeping her and her sister in the dark.

Juliette pulled from the kiss, tears shined in her eyes. "I love you, Kai."

Brianna jerked, realizing for the first time her father's name was not Death.

"And I you," He whispered, hoarsely. "Always."

"Then you must understand," she said as a tear fell down her cheek. She glanced at Brianna, giving her a small smile. "I have to fight for you and our children." She straightened her shoulders. "Remember, I am the daughter of Ares. He taught me well."

She pulled a long, glowing sword from the air in front of her, her body flickering before taking on her youthful form. Brianna gasped as she gazed at a woman who looked so much like her, they could be sisters.

Her mother's eyes met Brianna's. She nodded once and mouthed, *I love you.*

"I love you, too," she whispered.

She glanced toward death as his body flickered and she gazed upon his youthful form. He appeared only a few years older than her with his jaw squared and high cheekbones. His body had lost some softness and was more muscled. His blue eyes found hers as he nodded, reaching out his hand as a scythe appeared within it.

"Ahhh... There's the weird farming tool he chose as his weapon," Gabe said, rolling his eyes. "I hope he can battle with it."

Brianna frowned, tearing her eyes away from her father, finding her mother once again standing near the table. Brianna stepped toward her. The words the Fates were saying wrapped around her as she caught the last words.

"...of darkness will be mutinous to recover them and Death will be called to take her darkened soul to Hades for judgment."

The ground shook again as Brianna glanced at the tapestry on the table. Her heart lurched as she took in the images upon it, then complete darkness fell. Even before light flooded the area again, she knew what she would find.

She raised her eyes to find Kuraim gripping the arm of a woman. She had a beautiful face except for her gouged eyes. Snakes were in the place of her hair and her legs were replaced with a serpent's tail.

Through it all, the Fates continued to weave. Brianna saw that they weaved more than one tapestry, and Atropos had her scissors ready to cut the strings of life.

Gabe's voice broke her stare from the tapestries as the word he spoke echoed to her, broken and addled with guilt and love for someone who had never loved him back, sending an arrow of pain through her.

"Mum?" He whispered before darkness descended once again.

Chapter Thirty-One

The light returned again moments later. Gabe's white-blue gaze shifted from his mother to Kuraim. His teeth gritted as he took a step forward, but Kuraim drew a sword from the sheath at his back, stopping him.

"If you hurt her, I will rip you apart." Gabe's teeth were clenched so hard that his mouth barely moved.

"Gabe, don't," his mother pleaded, her words causing him to pause and stare at her with wide eyes. "I-I'm not worth your death...or your love. I've never been a mother to you, but perhaps, if I prevent your death, it will show the love I should have given you since your birth."

"Mum?" His voice was so strained he almost choked over the word.

"Enough of this display." Kuraim sneered. "You show love now because you've lost one of your gifts because your son blinded you."

She straightened. "I show this now because when he blinded me, he gave me back some of my humanity. Before I die, I will show him he's not worthless. In fact, he's priceless. I will right my wrongs *this* day."

An icy tear fell down Gabe's cheek.

Kuraim's eyes narrowed. "Sickening mortality. It weakens you and makes you even more despicable in my eyes."

"Perhaps." She raised her chin even though her words were weighted with sadness. "But he took away the blinders the serpent put in place. He gave me back my life, if only for a little while."

A growl rumbled from Kuraim's throat. Gabe took a step forward, but Brianna gripped his hand. If he went up against Kuraim alone, she had no doubt he would die.

"Why her?" Brianna asked, gaining Kuraim's attention.

"Oh, Little Goddess," he said, licking his bottom lip as his eyes swept over her. "You should know the answer. Two souls for the price of one death. The mortal and the serpent. Two times the power I can absorb."

Her eyes widened, realizing why he wanted the souls. He wanted them for their power. If he killed the gods, he could become one with more power than any god had ever possessed. For a moment, she wondered why he hadn't absorbed the other souls, but she knew. They didn't have enough power. Their gifts were minor. He viewed them as trash.

He moved closer to Gabe's mother, caressing her face as if he were a lover. "Seeing you now, Brianna, I understand why you've brought two dragons to their knees." His eyes darkened to black as he gazed at her. "I may keep you alive so I can break you the way you broke them."

A growl burst from Gabe, and Brianna realized his dragon was near. Kuraim grinned at his outburst as he leaned into Gabe's mother.

"I love you, Gabe," she whispered.

Kuraim inhaled deeply. The life drained from her body. Her corpse dropped at his feet. The snakes on her head gave one final hiss as her souls hovered in front of Kuraim's face.

Death reached forward. The souls changed course and glided into Death's hand. Kuraim's enraged glare met the blue eyes of Death.

"Did you really think I would allow you to gain souls in my presence?" Death asked, raising his chin. "All souls come to me in my presence to be delivered to Hades for judgment and her darkened soul will face him, not you. As will every soul here."

Kuraim raised his arms, his followers appearing behind him. "Then I must kill you first."

Brianna's eyes widened as she recognized people within his army. It wasn't a surprise to see Mrs. Colton, her sneer catching on Brianna and Gabe. Her gaze moved to Neva and Mr. Leo, then to Aidan and Alona. As Aidan's eyes settled on his mother's dead body, his face darkened. He raised his eyes to Gabe's, guilt flashing within them.

"Her death is on your hands," Gabe ground out, finally losing control of his dragon.

Aidan's eyes widened, and he unleashed his dragon. The two brothers flew above the armies, clashing in a great burst of fire and ice, starting the battle.

BRIANNA FROZE, BREAKING her gaze away from Gabe and Aidan's fight as the words of the Fates came to her again. "Evil becomes good and good becomes evil."

She frowned, confused.

Greer broke through the crowd fighting in front of her and stepped beside Brianna, a ball of fire in her hand, ready to fight.

"The fates spoke the prophecy out of order," Brianna said, her eyes sliding over Greer's tense expression.

"The prophecies aren't always spoken in the order of events." She glanced at the table where the Fates continued to weave, then scanned the crowd for attackers.

A bright light shining beside Kuraim pulled her gaze from them. An angel appeared, his wings outstretched. His fierce but beautiful face scanned the battle with a grin.

"What the hell? That's Aidan's father, Trustin," Greer frowned as her breaths quickened. "What's he doing here?"

"Welcome, my friend," Kuraim said as Brianna's eyes widened and Greer gasped.

"No," Greer breathed as if the breath had been knocked out of her.

"He has an angel on his side?" Brianna asked, shocked.

"He'll fall after this," Greer explained, her eyes shadowed by pain that Brianna didn't understand. "But it clarifies why Aidan sided with Kuraim."

A chilly wind settled over them and Brianna turned to stare into eyes the same shade as Gabe's. She furrowed her brows. The man before her was an angel, yet not. He possessed Gabe's nose, strong jaw, and white-blond hair, but black wings fell from his back, curving around Greer and Brianna as if protecting them from those who would attack them.

"Leonardo?" Greer's eyes narrowed in suspicion.

"I arrived just as Laurel died," he said, glancing at the crumpled body of Gabe's mother. His eyes darkening for a moment. "When I saw Trustin arrive, I realized if an angel can help evil," he said, his voice hard but a small smile played across his lips, "a fallen can help the side of good, especially in order to protect his son."

"You're Gabe's father," Brianna stated, knowing it to be true.

He smirked, and she instantly saw Gabe within it. "Hello, daughter-in-law. We'll catch up on pleasantries later. First, I must dispose of a crooked angel."

His wings spread out. Pumping them powerfully, he flew into the angel. Leonardo and Trustin clashed as two of Kuraim's followers advanced toward Brianna and Greer.

GREER THREW THE BALL of fire at the first banshee to reach them. Ares stepped in front of them, his sword arching, cutting a creature that resembled a lion in two, showing its human form to be that of Mr. Leo. Ares moved toward Brianna and unsheathed a sword, tossing it to her. She gripped it, finding it heavy, before glancing up at her grandfather with wide eyes. Golden light laced up her arm.

"It's your goddess' weapon," he said, smiling. "Enchanted to be used by you, and you alone. Allow it to do its job."

Brianna looked at it, trying to understand, then felt an overwhelming need to thrust it forward. As she did, a harpy fell on the end of her sword, impaling her. Her body became rigid before turning to dust.

Brianna smiled at Ares. "Thank you, Grandfather."

He grinned, pride shining in his eyes, and nodded. "Use it well."

A growl broke through Brianna's mind. She glanced up, finding Gabe and Aidan fighting above them. Fire and ice met in a never-ending match, neither of them gaining the upper hand.

Ares placed his hand on her shoulder. "Now, I must ask you to do something you might not understand." He glanced at the dragons once more. "You have to stop them, Brianna. You can't allow Gabe to kill Aidan."

"How am I going to do that when Gabe is so angry with him?" She asked and then bit on her bottom lip to keep it from trembling. "*Why* would I do that? He is part of Kuraim's army and Kuraim just killed their mother."

He lowered his voice. "He's *not* part of Kuraim's army, Brianna. He's part of mine." Brianna stared at her grandfather, aghast. Greer glanced at Ares, confused, as she threw another ball of fire at a werewolf. "He's my spy. If Gabe kills him, he will live with that guilt forever."

Brianna's eyes widened as Greer paled, shaken by the news. "I'll repeat...How the hell do you expect me to stop him?" She asked, shaking her head. "He's pissed off for good reason."

"Fuck," Greer said, shocking Brianna with the curse as she disposed of yet another banshee. She met her eyes, guilt sliding over her expression. "Will you do anything to help Gabe?"

Her stomach twisted as she realized whatever Greer was thinking, it was going to be bad. Still, it may be their only choice to cut through Gabe's anger at his brother long enough to explain Aidan's true position in the battle. "Of course, I will."

Greer winced. "Please, forgive me, Brianna. It's the only thing I could think of." A ball of fire lit in her hand. "Remember to scream louder than it hurts."

Before Brianna was able to react, Greer reared back and threw the ball of fire. White-hot pain slid through her. She didn't have to fake the scream.

Gabe threw one more spear of ice at Aidan, slicing through the scales on his side, and landed between Greer and Brianna. Immediately, he shifted. Gabe stood there naked. His stormy gaze was situated on Greer as the golden glow of a warrior lit his skin.

"You'll pay for that, witch," he said, baring his fangs. Brianna, still in pain, opened her mouth to stop him, but before she could speak, he lunged toward Greer.

Chapter Thirty-Two

"I will fucking fry you, Gabe," Greer said as a ball of fire lit in her hand.

Brianna bent over, trying to breathe through the pain, her sword still in her hand. As she took a wobbling step in their direction, she saw Mrs. Colton out of the corner of her eye, charging. She straightened as healthy skin weaved over her burned flesh. Gripping the sword tightly, she spun, arching the sword toward her old math teacher. Gabe turned toward them. Ice slid from his mouth, freezing Mrs. Colton as she jumped toward Brianna just as her sword sliced through Mrs. Colton's abdomen, shattering her body.

Gabe's eyes turned back to Greer, a snarl curling his upper lip. Brianna placed a hand on his shoulder, making his back straighten. "Gabe, it's not what you think."

Gabe shook his head. "I saw—"

"I was stopping you from killing your brother in the only way that I could." Greer blew out a breath, the fire in her hand dying out. "Everyone knows you will protect Brianna above anything else."

"Why would you protect him?" Gabe clenched his fists at his sides. "Are you with Kuraim?"

Greer straightened, insulted. "Absolutely not."

"Aidan is my spy," Ares said as he approached. "He's never been a part of Kuraim's army."

"But he allowed our mother to die." Gabe's body shook with anger, obviously having trouble controlling his dragon.

"He didn't know," Ares said, gently. "Kuraim didn't inform him. I suspect that he's lost trust in Aidan and knows he's a spy."

"Then that means he's in danger," Greer said, her face paling as her body trembled. Brianna raised a brow. Now and then, she wondered if Greer's crush on Aidan was more intense than what Greer usually showed.

Gabe twisted his head toward his brother, now facing off with Kuraim as he protected Juliette. In that instant, he understood Aidan wasn't the enemy. With a growl, his dragon burst from him as he made his way to protect the brother he thought had betrayed him.

The Fate's voices broke through the battle. "The killer of the Gods where one must stand, and one must fall, facing many betrayals."

Brianna's eyes landed on Neva and Alona, who smirked as they watched Aidan and Kuraim face off. With sudden clarity, she realized they were the ones who informed Kuraim of Aidan's betrayal.

Her eyes widened as she realized. *Betrayals*...One of them was going to fall.

She gripped her sword and ran forward, slashing her way toward them, hoping she could prevent the words of a prophecy and change the pattern in the Fate's hands.

KURAIM'S EYES NARROWED at the two dragons before him. Brianna kept her eyes on the sword in her hands as she slashed into a minotaur, blocking her way. His body fell with a thud. She jumped over it, already turning to ash as her mother's sword dropped to the ground.

The Fate's words came again. "One will live, one will fall."

She ran to her mother's side as Kuraim thrust forward, slicing into Gabe's chest. Brianna's cry of anguish echoed through the battle as he fell, returning to his human form. Brianna stumbled to a stop, her soul crying out.

"One will stand...One will cry," The Fates said as a tear fell down her cheek. Aidan's head bowed over his brother in his naked human form.

Kuraim walked forward, a sneer on his face. Brianna raised her sword. In her anger and grief, she was weak. She knew that. She faced him, his smile cocky as he advanced, his eyes firmly on her. She didn't dare break eye contact as she faced him, but sensed her mother move away from her.

"The battle is over, Little Goddess," he purred, his eyes boring into hers as he drew closer.

Brianna's hands shook around the handle of her sword as she raised it, ready to slice him in two. Instead, he lurched forward, as the life faded from his eyes. Brianna's gaze moved to Juliette, who had slammed her sword to the hilt into his darkened heart from behind. She glared, placing her foot on his back, pulling her sword free. His black blood dripped from it as he fell at her feet.

"You're right," Juliette said, her voice grim. "The battle *is* over."

His soul hovered over him before it glided into Death's hand and Brianna fell to her knees beside the dragon shifter she had fallen in love with.

AFTER THEIR LEADER'S death, Kuraim's followers dropped their weapons and fled. Bodies and ash of the dead littered the ground. Blood soaked into the soil, but the only one that mattered to Brianna was Gabe.

"Declarations and screams," The Fates said as they continued to weave. Atropos lifted her scissors.

Brianna cried out as she pulled Gabe's body toward her, her tears dripping onto his beloved face.

"Goddess..." he whispered weakly, reaching up to trace her cheek with his fingertips. She could feel the warmth in them. For an ice dragon, she realized that meant death was near.

"Please don't leave me," she choked out, the words crushing her heart and soul. "Please...I love you."

Gabe took a deep, shuddering breath. "Don't cry...Goddess." His voice was barely a whisper as he struggled to speak. "Your smile...is what I...want...to take...with me."

"Gabe," she cried his name. "Please don't leave me. Please."

A shudder wracked through his body and his eyes closed. She cried out, pulling him closer as Atropos readied her scissors.

"Atropos, don't," she begged, unable to imagine a world without Gabe. It would be empty...pointless.

The Fates' words whispered over her. "Love conquers all but can destroy."

Juliette's eyes filled with tears as she faced her daughter. "Do you truly love him?"

Brianna's bottom lip quivered, and she nodded. "More than my life. I can't let him go."

A tear fell down Juliette's cheek as Atropos readied her scissors to cut Gabe's string of life. Juliette spun toward her.

"Stop, Atropos," she ordered, straightening. Death moved toward Juliette. Confusion crossed Atropos' face. "You know this isn't the path he's on."

Atropos nodded, her scissors moving away as Death faced Juliette. She took his cheeks in her hands, her lips meeting his.

"I love you, Kai," she whispered against them. "I always have."

Confusion crossed his face. "I love you, too."

She took a deep breath. "But I love our daughter more."

"As do I," he said, his eyes darkening in worry.

Juliette turned to Greer. "You know what to do."

The Fates chanted. "You will bring Death to his knees when a decision is made. A choice of one and magic will be found in words."

As Greer stepped forward, tears falling down her cheeks, understanding crossed Death's face.

A chill slid down Brianna's spine as her father screamed, "No!"

Chapter Thirty-Three

"Mom?" Brianna's voice was hoarse as tears slid down her face. Her stomach churned, warning her that something was about to happen...Something bad. She swallowed over a lump in her throat.

"Returning and retreating, the souls must be saved. Many will fall, many will fail and many will die." The Fates' voices reflected such sadness that it resonated through everyone around them. The soul's white orbs flew toward Death, searching out the one who would take them to the river, Styx and Charon's boat, where they would be taken for judgment for the payment of drachmas. He inhaled sharply, unable to move as the souls of the fallen hit him in the chest, absorbing into him. His body glowed with them, yet they kept coming, preventing him from moving toward the woman he loved. Juliette gave him one last look of longing.

Greer's voice lifted over them. Her words seemed as if they were forced from her. "Vitam enim madatum est a madatum est a vita Hecate! Nos hanc accipere sacrificium!"

"What does that mean?" Brianna asked, fear settling into her soul.

"A life for a life on the command of Hecate," Leonardo translated softly, his voice dripping in despair as he limped toward Brianna, his gaze on his son as tears fill his eyes. "We accept this sacrifice."

"A life for a life?" Brianna asked, terrified, as her gaze found her mother's.

Greer fell to her knees, sobbing, the spell done as Brianna's mother picked up her sword, the truth making itself known. "I love you, Brianna," she choked out. "I do this for you, but I also do it to save everyone. You and Gabe must live for that. You will understand soon."

Brianna opened her mouth to ask what she meant, but the Fates' words came again. "Where Aphrodite's blood cries as one lives and one falls to doom."

Her eyes widened as she took in her mother's sword, understanding what her mother was about to do. "Mom, no!" she screamed as Juliette ran her sword through her body, and Atropos raised her scissors and cut the thread on her mother's life.

"Declarations and screams," the Fates continued. "Both unheard until the breath is taken."

Juliette's blood dripped down the hilt, soaking into the ground. Gabe suddenly took a deep breath, his wounds weaving together. His eyes opened to stare into Brianna's with such despair and love that her aching heart reached for him while it grieved for her mother.

GABE REACHED UP AND touched the tear on her cheek, his eyes sliding over her face. "I heard you, Goddess," he whispered in awe. "I thought I was dead, but I heard you say you loved me."

"I do," she said, sobbing. She trembled with the force of her emotions, grief for her mother, relief that Gabe was alive, love for him, and immense guilt because her mother had sacrificed herself so they could be together.

"Then why are you crying?" He frowned, sitting up slowly.

He tore his gaze away from her, taking in the surrounding carnage. His eyes fell first on Greer, sobbing uncontrollably, then, upon the woman she was bent over...Juliette.

"No..." He looked at the cloaked figure of Death, fallen upon his knees. He was crawling toward the woman he loved, unable to stand in his grief, reaching for her and pulling her into his arms as he sobbed, kissing her face, and begging for her not to leave him.

"She was alive when I fell," Gabe whispered. "What happened?"

"She gave her life for you," Leonardo said, his voice strained.

Gabe blinked as he took in his father's face, realizing he was part of the battle for the first time.

"Father?" Gabe's voice was filled with so many emotions as he took in the man's face he had only seen a handful of times since his birth.

He shook his head, pushing away the rage and confusion at his presence. "Gave her life for me? She wouldn't do that."

He turned to Brianna, taking in her shattered expression. Tears streamed down her face as she nodded. Horror washed over his face. "W-Why?"

"F-For me," Brianna sobbed, her shoulders shaking. "Sh-She did it for me."

Gabe shook his head, searching for another explanation as the Fates spoke again. "Only this sacrifice will save them all."

Hera stepped forward, her beautiful face streaked with tears and her gown soaked with blood. "She didn't simply do it for you," she said, softly. "She did it for all of us. She was helping fix the mistake I made when I refused Death and Juliette's marriage. I upset the balance of darkness and light when I forced them away from each other. By doing that, I put the world in danger."

Brianna shook her head. "She asked me if I loved him. That's why she did this."

"No, child. She was going to make that sacrifice, anyway. It is no fault of yours or Gabe's. It is mine." She shifted as her bottom lip trembled. "Soulmates are perfectly balanced and have destinies even the Fates do not know. Only the Oracle has the insight, but often it is cloaked in mystery. When it is unbalanced, blood from a willing hand must be sacrificed to right it. My refusal of her marriage with Death didn't help matters. When I forced them apart, I changed their destinies. You see, there is something that is destined for the soulmates to do. Hades and Persephone balanced the Underworld with light and dark. Death and Juliette were meant to balance something else, and you and Gabe will balance the world in another way. Whatever their destiny was, I prevented it. Now, the balance is on your shoulders, and we must do everything we can to make sure that destiny is reached. Your mother died to save us all."

Brianna's eyes narrowed. "This is *your* fault." Her voice shook with anger. "Your need for revenge killed my mother."

Hera trembled as tears continued to fall down her cheeks. "I am responsible, and I will take the consequences of my actions from here until the mistakes are mended."

The Fates spoke again, but Brianna didn't break the glare she was sending toward Hera. She was angry that her actions had caused such devastation to everyone around them. Though she didn't want to hear anymore, the Fates' words wrapped around her again.

"For some, death will be a permanence. For some, it will not, but it's not all Death's choice who goes and who stays."

Death's screams echoed through the air. Brianna swung toward him, only to be met with the horror of her mother's body fading in her father's arms.

Hades stepped forward, his blue eyes dark. "She's gone. Son, you know I can't be unbiased when judging Juliette." He frowned. "And you can't carry her soul to judgment. We're too close to her. She's gone to another realm where her soul will be judged fairly."

"Which one?" Death cried, his pleading gaze meeting his father's.

"I wasn't told." Hades whispered, bowing his head. "But we will find out, then meet with the god or goddess of that realm."

Her mother's death, the pain of almost losing Gabe, and the anger at Hera became too much. Brianna began to sob as the weight of it all settled upon her.

Gabe pulled her into his arms as his father's dark gaze settled upon him. Gabe met his eyes, taking in the sorrow there and knowledge that frightened him more than anything. His stomach churned, sensing whatever Leonardo knew would only bring doom for him and for the woman he held in his arms. The woman he would sacrifice anything for.

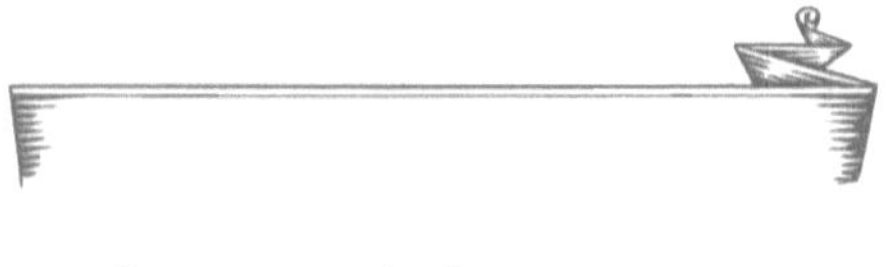

Chapter Thirty-Four

Greer was inconsolable as Brianna rose to stare into the eyes of the girl who had spoken the spell to allow her mother to die in the place of Gabe. Gabe stood beside her, his brows furrowed as his father conjured a white robe from thin air. He pulled it on, covering his naked form before standing beside Brianna, wishing he could offer her comfort when he knew there was none to be had. His own mother's death weighed heavily on him...Her last words shredding through him as he wondered what she would have been like if she remained human.

Brianna stood in front of Greer, silent, her face strained as she struggled to speak to the girl she had considered her friend. Slowly, Greer closed her eyes before opening them again, her expression holding so much remorse and grief that the force of it circled them like a snake, constricting their air.

"I didn't want to kill her," Greer said, her voice breaking. "My grandmother compelled me before the fight began. I didn't even remember I was supposed to do the spell until J-Juliette told me I knew what to do."

"Greer..." Brianna's voice was almost a whisper and so broken that Gabe stepped closer to her on instinct to protect her.

"I-I'm so sorry," Greer wailed, her eyes moving to Death, who still knelt, looking at his empty hands and sobbing. How could they do this to her? To Greer? To her father?

She didn't understand as Greer spoke to Death. "That damn prophecy...I told you I didn't want to hurt you, but they made sure I did in the end, didn't they?"

"It needed to be done," Hecate said, walking toward them. Until that moment, she had remained hidden. The guilt and remorse on her face blending as she glanced at her granddaughter.

"What do you mean?" Brianna asked, her hands clenching at her sides with tears flowing down her cheeks as she faced the goddess who made sure that Greer fulfilled a prophecy she had fought so hard against.

"The Fates...They drew the lots and called your mother because they didn't line up with what the prophecies had foretold. The lots told the Fates Gabe was the one who would die, but that didn't make sense and the prophecies have to be fulfilled." Hecate's eyes filled with tears. "So, we looked at them again. Someone from Aphrodite's bloodline would have to die. The prophecies even gave a clue as to who that would be because their death would bring Death to his knees. Greer was the one who asked the question, and the only way to fulfill the prophecy and keep Gabe alive was if Juliette sacrificed herself and Greer was the one who worked the spell. A life for a life."

"She shouldn't have sacrificed herself for me," Gabe insisted, but even speaking those words hurt Brianna. She wasn't telling a lie when she told her mother she loved him more than her own life.

"She didn't do it just for you." Hecate raised her chin. "Or even for Brianna, though her love for you did give her the strength to do it. Only her sacrifice will save us all...That was part of the prophecy. Juliette wanted to know why, so she called The Oracle and received another prophecy. The balances of day and night and light and dark bound together...The heroes must not turn to dust, or the world will follow. The prophecy was plain. You both will save the world."

Brianna inhaled sharply as she glanced at Gabe. His brow was furrowed, a thin layer of ice on his skin as an icy tear fell down his cheek. "And how are we to save the world?"

Hecate took a deep breath. "I don't know, but I do know for you to do it, you must be alive. So did Juliette."

Brianna's eyes moved from Hecate to Greer before turning toward her father, but then her gaze caught on Hera's as her face darkened. Something flashed in her expression that caused Brianna to frown, but as soon as it appeared, it was gone, and Brianna convinced herself that she had imagined it.

NIGHT HAD FALLEN. HERA stood in her orchard, her hair blowing softly behind her as she glanced at Ladon in his human form. Close to seven feet tall, his tanned skin glistened in the moonlight. Jet-black hair fell over one amber tinted eye. He was handsome...She would never deny that, and her heart did beat for Ladon as well as Zeus.

Being in love with two men was one of the hardest things Hera had faced in her life. If that secret became known, one would kill the other. She wouldn't allow that. Maybe that was the true reason for her bitterness with Aphrodite and Juliette. She could never be truly happy without both bound to her.

"A year and a day," she said, clenching her fists. "How am I supposed to right my wrongs when there is that stupid rule? I have to grant Brianna and Gabe's annulment if they request it on that day. Zeus made sure of that to limit my power."

"You're sure they'll show up?" Ladon's brow furrowed.

She shook her head. "I can't risk the chance they will. My silly granddaughter has all these ideas of how love is supposed to happen." She shook her head as tears fell down her cheeks. "It's my fault. Juliette had to raise her in the mortal realm, Brianna's powers bound until she came of age, all because I forced Juliette to marry that mortal."

"The shades may have an answer."

"I don't want them to die," she groaned in frustration. "That would be counterproductive to what I'm trying to do."

"I didn't say they would die, but it will be painful for both of them. Even if it's temporary, being separated from the one you are bound to is torture. It may drive them insane."

Hera's heart clenched. Could she do that to Brianna after she vowed to fix the mess she made by doing the same to her own granddaughter?

She met Ladon's gaze and, though she hated the choice she had to make, she nodded. "Call the shades. Tell them what they must do."

"Yes, My Goddess." A moment later, his dragon burst from him, and he left the orchard for the first time in centuries.

She watched him fly away, then strolled through the garden. Her lips trembled as she glanced at the apples hanging from the trees. A gust of wind told her she was not alone. The sandalwood scent of her husband surrounded her.

"Zeus," she whispered before he stepped from behind a tree, his eyes narrowed.

"What was Ladon doing in his human form?" He questioned.

She sighed heavily. Though her jealousy was known throughout many stories, they somehow did not reflect that Zeus was ten times worse.

"I needed to speak with him so he could do an errand for me."

"You know I've ordered him not to shift into his human form." He ground out from between his clenched teeth.

She crossed her arms. "And *you* know, he is the one being in Olympus you have no control over. I am his goddess, but you are not his god. I choose what orders he listens to and which orders to give."

"*You* still have to listen to *my* orders." Zeus said, stepping closer to her. "What was so important that you went against them?"

"Righting my wrongs." Her eyes flashed as she faced her husband. "It was worth your ire, dear husband."

Zeus' nostrils flared. "Do you want him to die?"

Hera's soul shook with the thought of Ladon ceasing to exist. "You know I don't."

"Then keep your distance from the dragon, Hera," he said, the muscles of his jaw flexing. "Don't force me to end his life."

Then he was gone. Blowing out a breath, she stared up at the apples above her, reaching up to pluck a deep red apple from the tree that would take the ability to kill Ladon away from Zeus as she whispered, "Don't force me to make sure you can't, dear husband."

Chapter Thirty-Five

Gabe stared out the window of their room in Aphrodite's home. The beautiful skyline of Olympus did nothing for him as worry gnawed at him for his soulmate...His wife. She had slept since arriving, barely saying a word to him, but his mind was filled with her voice as he lay dying saying that she loved him...Pleading for his life to continue.

He was sure that love would fade. It had cost her so much...Her mother's life...She would never see her again. Worse, her mother's soul and body were in another realm and no one knew where that was.

He loved her. He didn't deny that...At least to himself. His shame kept him from admitting it to her. Though a god now, he was unworthy. No matter how much he tried to shed the image as the son of a fallen and a gorgon, it would follow him. It made him question himself, but more than anything, it made him question her safety. How much would she give up for him? He worried it would be her life.

"Gabe?" Her broken, gritty voice made him clench a hand to his chest. Even though he loved her, he knew he shouldn't allow her to continue in a relationship with him that would hurt her to the point of her hating him. But he was a selfish bastard. He would cling to her, even if it was only as her guardian.

"I'm here, Goddess," he said, not turning to her yet as he tried to prepare himself for her heartbroken tears.

"Why haven't you come to bed?" She whispered. He could feel her gaze upon him.

"I've been thinking about my death." He swallowed because he had to face what she had spoken. He couldn't ignore it. "You told me you love me."

Fighting tears, he turned to face her. Her eyes were wide, and though he could see the love clearly, he knew it would fade eventually when she continued to lose those she loved because of him.

"I do love you." She reached for him, but he moved away from her. If he felt her touch, he wouldn't say what he needed to.

"You shouldn't." He shook his head, his voice cracking as he spoke. "I destroy everything. It's in my nature."

She tilted her head. "You haven't destroyed me."

"I will." An icy tear fell down his cheek as he spoke the only lie he would speak to her. "But I don't think it matters. I don't think you truly love me. It's an infatuation that is strengthened by our bond. In the moment of my death, you simply were overcome by it and didn't want me to die."

"You're wrong, Gabe." She lifted her chin.

He knew he was breaking her heart, but she needed to distance herself from him so he could save her...Because he did love her and he would not allow her to be harmed because of him, and even though it killed him, there was still a part of him that believed she would find someone better.

"You think what you feel for me is being in love? You don't know what being in love truly is. It isn't about the sweet stuff...the kisses, the hugs and the whispers in your ear. It's about all the gritty things too...the arguments, the heartache, or when the person you are in love with is gone or dealing with their insufferable days." Her chin was still raised, tears rested in her eyes as he continued. "Believe me, what you're feeling right now will eventually wear off and you will see me the same way everyone else does. I'll annoy you and you will probably end up hating things about me. Hell...You'll probably hate me, period." A tear fell down her cheek, but he forced himself to continue. "I don't look forward to that day, because when it happens, it will kill a part of my soul to see your beautiful, bright eyes dim when you look at me because I get up for that look in your eyes. I take the next step for it and when it's gone, only the memory of it will help me go on. But I want you to know that even when that fades and the illusion of being in love with me is gone, I will still go forward and I will do that because I know even then, you may need me and when you do, no matter if you hate me with a thousand deaths, I will do anything you want. Because even knowing that you may hate me and that sparkle in your eyes will fade, I want to help you. I will *always* want to help you. I don't need you in love with me for that. I just need you to remember, even when you start to hate me, I will be there for you. Even when you figure out that I'm not the one who has lit your soul on fire, I will do anything to make sure you are okay. That's all I need. As long as you can give me that, Goddess, it will be okay. I will be okay."

She straightened, the fire in her eyes flashing with immense strength and a stubborn will that could break even him. "You're afraid." Her nostrils flared, causing him to flinch. "You're trying to push me away. I won't allow you to do that. I *do* love you, Gabe. I will always be in love with you and no matter what you say or do, I will always know that you *are* the one who sets my soul on fire. You may be my other half, but I know exactly why my soul cried for yours. I have always loved you in the abyss and now. Maybe you don't feel the same. Maybe that's why you are pushing me away, but whether you feel the same or not, it doesn't make my feelings any less real."

He took a shuddering breath. "There is someone better for you, Goddess."

She shook her head. "No, there never will be."

She stepped close to him and pressed her lips to his. He closed his eyes, pulling her closer to him. His tongue swept into her mouth, and he knew that she was his. He could only hope that he wouldn't hurt her anymore than he already had.

THE INSTANT SOMEONE entered their room, Gabe sensed it, opening his eyes. He rolled away from Brianna while still staying close in case of danger. He narrowed his eyes as the shadows blended with the surrounding darkness.

They only narrowed further as his father stepped toward him. "I see you've mended things with your goddess...for now," he said, his eyes sweeping over her sleeping form. Gabe shifted closer to her.

"What do you want and how did you know about that little...tiff?" Gabe asked, frowning when Brianna didn't move.

He raised a brow. "I was an angel once. I still have some of my gifts. For example, your goddess sleeps soundly. She will not wake until our chat is over. She will remain unharmed."

"Why are you here?" Gabe asked through his teeth.

"I realize you're angry with me, Gabe, but I promise what is about to happen is for your good, and hers." He straightened his shoulders. "It's for the good of us all."

A prickle of fear shot down Gabe's spine. "What are you talking about?"

"You have to remain married after the year and a day," Leonardo said, casting his gaze toward Brianna. "In order for that to happen, you must not show up on the day that marks your year and a day to ask for an annulment."

"You can't ask me not to do that," Gabe said, glancing at Brianna. She wanted a normal, real relationship, and he knew now he would not be able to deny her anything.

He sighed. "I'm sorry, son. I'm not asking."

Darkness fell around him as his father's voice deepened. "By the order of Hera, Queen of the Gods, you will be imprisoned by the shades of the underworld until the year and a day has passed.

Afterward, Hera won't be obliged to accept your plea to end your marriage."

Gabe tried to move, but the shades wrapped around him, suffocating him as they pulled him down, down, down. His mind and heart screamed for Brianna until he fell into a cave. His father had followed and stood in front of him with his coal-black wings outstretched.

The shades moved away from him and immediately, Gabe advanced on his father, his dragon flashing beneath his skin, but he found he was unable to shift. "Take me back!" he screamed, desperate as he regretted every single word he'd said to her that night. He should have told her he loved her instead of pushing her away. "She's going to think I left her."

"We'll tell her after your year and a day has passed." Leonardo raised his brows. "She'll be informed of what happened here."

But she could find someone else in that time.

The thought tortured his mind as he fell to his knees. A pain like no other slid through him as he prepared himself to beg a father who had never cared for him. Before he could release one pleading word from between his lips, Leonardo was gone, leaving Gabe screaming out for Brianna in the darkness of the Underworld.

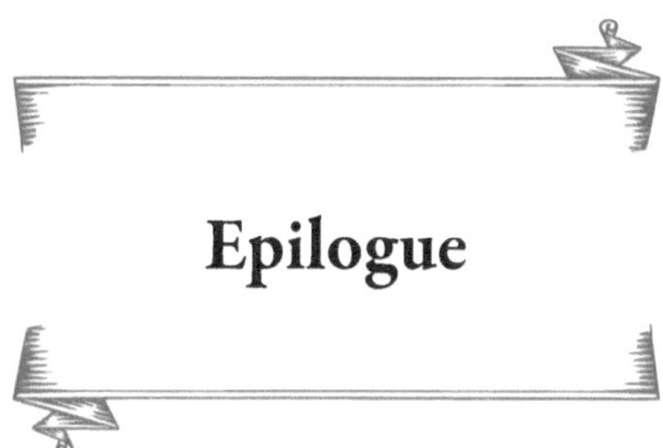

Epilogue

Nine Months later

Gabe was on his knees, his icy tears falling down his face as he prayed to the gods. He'd said a million prayers to every god and goddess he could think of since he'd been there. As the darkness surrounded him, he thought of Nyx, and the prayer to her fell from his lips. Brianna filled his mind, torturing him all these months. Every day, every minute, brought a new desperation to return to her, but he was beginning to lose hope. He was beginning to wish for death if he could not be near her.

He had heard the shades murmuring, increasing his desperation. They weren't going to let him go. They fed off despair and his was addictive, feeding their need for darkness every second of the day.

He fell back to the dirty floor of the cave, lying flat upon it as the prayer finished. Tears continued to leak from his eyes. "Please...Please, someone help me." His voice was hoarse from all the tears he had cried and all the times he had screamed Brianna's name.

The shadows shifted. A woman with pale skin and bright blue eyes stepped in front of him. Her long, dark hair moved to the side as her body pulsed with magic.

"My grandmother sent me to assist you," she said, smiling compassionately. "My name is Vera, granddaughter of Nyx."

Gabe blinked as he sat up, trying to decide if this was a dream or if he had finally been heard. "How was she able to hear me in the Underworld?"

"She visits the Underworld occasionally. She heard your cries for your soulmate. Now, I am here to ask, how can I assist you?"

He licked his parched lips. "Brianna...I need her." His body trembled. "She needs me. She needs to know I was brought here because of Hera. I didn't leave her. I love her."

"Brianna, the granddaughter of Hades?" She asked, a sparkle in her eyes.

"Yes, my...my wife," he said, clutching his chest, the word slicing through him because he failed her.

"You're the one she's been mourning," she said with a sigh. The pain of knowing Brianna had been hurt by his absence was suffocating. The fact he caused it was unbearable.

"Please...Take me from here." He rose to his knees, clasping his hands in front of him.

"I can't," she said. "I am not allowed. Only the family of Hades can do that, but I can let them know you're here."

"No...Don't let Brianna come to this place," he whispered, afraid the shades would attack her. "Send her father or grandfather."

Vera tilted her head again as she studied him. Her eyes turned white for a moment before returning to their normal blue. "I can't prevent her from coming to you. I think she's supposed to. You can't prevent destiny, only help it."

Gabe nodded as he realized the only way he would be with her again was if she traveled to him. He had to believe she was strong enough to make the journey. He had to believe in her strength.

"Bring my wife to me," he said, his voice breaking. "Please keep her safe."

Vera smiled, brightening the whole cave because, within it, there was hope for him and for Brianna. "Don't worry, dragon," she said, softly. "Your soul will be whole again...As will hers. I promise I will be with her the whole time, keeping her safe."

Then she faded. Gabe closed his eyes, hoping her appearance wasn't a dream and he would see Brianna again soon.

Acknowledgements:

Thank you so much to my children, Josh, Izzie and Constance and my grandchildren Maggie and Slade. Also, thank you to my mother, Kaye Russell Hirjak and my step-dad, Paul Hirjak. Also, so much appreciation to my sisters, Kara, Amber, Sandra and Chastity and to my brothers, James and Robert. A huge thank you to my cousins, Aree Rayne Marlow, Rebecca Grieshaber (Thank you for naming your child after Gabe! That is such an honor!) and Christopher Russell. Also, thank you to my Uncles Jason, Terry and Anthony and my Aunt Wanda. I have a huge amount of love and thanks to Vera Hollins. Thank you so much to my friends, Hopi and Alvin Craig, Connie Sanchez, Krista Clark Follis, Terri Trexler, Cindy Rose-Fryman, Valerie Rose, Jenny Willis, Maria Zamudo, Berenice Quinones and Melinda Sanchez. Also, thanks to Xavier Sanchez for cheering me on. Also, a big thank you to my grandmother, Mildred Hardy. Last but not least, I would like to thank my readers! I love you all! Thank you so much for being my biggest cheerleaders. You are all so wonderful.

Don't miss out!

Visit the website below and you can sign up to receive emails whenever Amanda Penn publishes a new book. There's no charge and no obligation.

https://books2read.com/r/B-A-RJZY-KBMKC

BOOKS 2 READ

Connecting independent readers to independent writers.

About the Author

Amanda Penn was born in Tullahoma, Tennessee where she developed a love for books and writing. Now living in Texas, she is the mother of three beautiful children and grandmother to two. She has been a published writer since 2012.